The Jackson M Chronic...

FORGED IN FIRE AND BLOOD

By
Angel Giacomo

1st Battalion
Publishing

Copyright ©

First publication in 2021 by 1st Battalion Publishing.
1stbattalionpublishing@gmail.com

ISBN 978-17345674-5-8

Original cover photograph by breakermaximus.
Breakermaximus.com
Licensed by iStock by Getty Images.
iStockphoto.com

Printed in the United States of America.

First Edition: 2021

DISCLAIMER-FICTION

Other than actual historical events and public figures, all characters and incidents portrayed in this novel are fictitious. Any resemblance to actual persons, living or dead, is purely coincidental.

DEDICATION

This book is dedicated to all who have served in every branch of the military. I write it with extreme humility. It is to honor the veterans of the United States who fought in our conflicts, both past, present, and future.

"A true leader has the confidence to stand alone, the courage to make tough decisions, and the compassion to listen to the needs of others. He does not set out to be a leader, but becomes one by the equality of his actions and the integrity of his intent." - General Douglas MacArthur

"Leaders are like eagles…they don't flock, you find them one at a time." – Knute Rockne

"I offer neither pay, nor quarters, nor food; I offer only hunger, thirst, forced marches, battles, and death. Let him who loves his country with his heart, and not merely with his lips, follow me." – Giuseppe Garibaldi

ACKNOWLEDGMENT

Thank you to those who have believed in me. Especially Sally Berneathy.

A shout out to Bradley Love and Amy Harden for their comments and suggestions.

An extra special thanks goes to Dr. Russell W. Ramsey, USMA 1957. Your stories of West Point have been interesting, enjoyable, and extremely helpful. This work is dedicated to you more than anyone else. Thank you for being my friend. Hooah!

CHAPTER 1

April 1, 1985 – Double M Ranch, Montana
0845 hours

Mangus and Jackson stepped out of the house after breakfast. Steam rolled off the dew on the porch rails. The blood-red sun blazed in the eastern sky.

Jackson took off his cowboy hat. He wiped his brow with his forearm and placed the hat back on his head. "What did mother nature do, forget spring entirely? It's almost eighty degrees already."

"I know." Mangus scraped his feet on the mat. "The weather guy said it'll push over ninety this afternoon. It got hot so fast the snow melted in two days. Now I have a yard full of mud. Where are you going today?"

"North pasture to check for new calves. Saw two cows ready to pop yesterday. I should be back by lunch."

"See you then." Mangus went back into the house.

Jackson strolled into the barn whistling *Doctor, Doctor*. He loved the lyrics. They reminded him of his girlfriend, the love of his life, Cathy.

His horse, Bandit, stomped his white-socked front feet and neighed.

"Hi, yourself, knucklehead." Jackson pulled the lead rope from a peg outside Bandit's stall. "Ready to go?"

Bandit bounced his chestnut head up and down so fast his white blaze blurred.

"Me too." Jackson tied Bandit to the wall and saddled him. He went to the tack room to grab his snake chaps and put one leg on. *No way. Too hot. If I wear those, I'll have pink lotion on my legs tonight for an itchy rash. No, thank you.* He took them off.

The sun climbed higher in the sky as Jackson rode across the north pasture.

"Moo…"

Jackson pulled back on the reins and glanced around. Outside a small thicket stood a brown and white Hereford cow. Bloody afterbirth lay between her legs.

"Moo…"

Jackson climbed off his horse. "Where's your baby?" *Hope the wolves didn't get it.*

Leaves rustled. A small brown and white head emerged from the brush.

"There you are. I see why you can't climb out, little one. Your feet are all tangled up." Knife in hand, Jackson approached the calf and bent over to cut a vine. He stepped back. Something moved under his boot heel.

"Ssssss…"

Burning pain jammed through his right calf. *Shit! Rattlesnake.* He went down, clutching his leg.

Bandit reared up and stomped the snake into red goo. He stayed at Jackson's side instead of running off.

Jackson removed his belt and snugged it tightly around his leg, right below the knee. Snakebite 101. Slow the flow of venom into his bloodstream. He climbed into the saddle with his right leg stuck straight out. To keep his heart from racing and spreading the poison further, he drew slow, deep breaths. *Panic is my enemy. It's good I learned how to calm my mind in the POW camp. The only useful thing to come out of the experience. Well, that and my friends.* He picked up the reins and clicked his tongue. "Take me home, boy."

Time slowed as Bandit followed the fence line. Jackson laid his head on the horse's neck to ease the strain on his back. His leg throbbed with his pulse. In twenty minutes, Bandit ambled into the area in front of the main house.

Mangus ran down the porch steps and grabbed the reins. "What's wrong?"

"Hit by a rattlesnake." Jackson pointed at his right calf.

"Jake, bring my Chevy over here!" Mangus yelled at a ranch hand with lead ropes slung over his shoulder.

"Yes, sir." The man dropped everything and sprinted for the driveway.

Jackson grabbed the saddle horn and eased himself slowly from Bandit's back to the ground.

Mangus threw his arm around Jackson's waist. "Easy. Put your arm across my shoulders. Let me take your weight."

"Okay." Jackson flopped his arm behind Mangus' neck and leaned against his side.

A red Chevy Suburban drove up beside them. Jake jumped out, opened the rear passenger door, and ran back to the driver's seat.

Mangus helped Jackson into the back seat then climbed in beside him. "Head to the hospital in Harve. I don't care about the speed limit. If the sheriff tries to pull us over, don't stop. I'll accept the ticket or any of the consequences, but only at the hospital."

"Yes, sir." Jake jammed on the gas pedal so hard the SUV skidded out of the driveway, throwing gravel in every direction.

Mangus slit the leg of Jackson's jeans with his pocketknife. "The fang marks in your calf are huge. The snake nailed you good." He cut the shank of Jackson's boot. Leather ripped as he sawed all the way to the sole.

"Those are my favorite pair. They're broke in perfectly." Jackson clenched his fists as electricity shot up his spine.

"Don't care. You're losing the circulation in your foot from the swelling."

Scrub brush and barbed wire fences rushed by the SUV's open windows. Hot wind blew the roar of an over-worked engine into the passenger compartment.

Jackson grabbed Mangus' hand. "I almost can't breathe." He sucked air into his lungs in short, quick breaths. "My face is numb." *I'm gonna die.*

Mangus leaned over the front seat. "Blow the engine if you have to. Get us to the damn hospital!"

"Oohhh…make it stop." Jackson gripped his chest, trying to breathe. Fiery agony enveloped him for the want of oxygen. He fought the screams behind his closed-off throat.

"Jackson. You're turning blue. Talk to me." Mangus rubbed Jackson's back.

"Feels like someone's twisting a red-hot poker in my leg." Jackson grabbed his head. "My head's about to explode." His stomach cramped and rolled. He heaved pink, frothy vomit onto the floorboards.

Mangus held him steady. "Easy, son. Why aren't we there yet? He's throwing up blood. Hurry."

Jake tapped the speedometer gauge. "We're at a hundred miles an hour. I can't make this thing go any faster. It's pegging at max RPMs now. The last sign said two miles. Be there in less than a minute."

The burned smell of abused brakes filled the Suburban as it slid to a stop in the emergency bay. A continuous hi-low obnoxious tone blasted from the horn as Jake pressed on the steering wheel.

Four people dressed in white ran outside. Two men and two women. One man pushed a gurney ahead of him.

"My son's been bitten by a rattlesnake!" Mangus eased Jackson's arm across his shoulders. "Easy. I've got you."

"Trying." Jackson set his feet on the ground. He leaned against his godfather. *It hurts.*

The man pushed a gurney alongside the Suburban.

"Owwww…" Jackson collapsed on it.

Mangus grabbed Jackson's hand.

"Make it stop." Jackson gripped his godfather's hand like a vice. Each bump of the gurney sent shivers of agony throughout his body. "Owww…" The attendant pushed him into a room full of bright lights.

A man in a white lab coat shoved Mangus back on his heels. "I'm Dr. Baker. You can't stay here. Go sign him in and take a seat in the waiting area. We'll take good care of him. What's his name?"

"Jackson. Don't let him die. Please. I can't lose him." Mangus chewed on his fingernails.

"I'll do my best." Dr. Baker pointed at the door. "But I can't with you in here."

Mangus kissed Jackson's forehead. "Don't you dare give up on me."

Jackson bit his tongue to focus through the discomfort. "I won't, but it hurts so much."

"Sara saw us leave."

"Oh, no." Jackson pictured his mad godmother, hands on her hips, saying *Jackson Joseph MacKenzie* in her growling Marine DI voice. The image helped to force himself to breathe.

Mangus ruffled Jackson's hair. "Yeah. Fight like you always do. I'll be right outside."

"Okay." Jackson dropped his head back on the pillow.

"Let's check the damage." Dr. Baker rotated Jackson's leg.

The movement sent an excruciating explosion up his spine. Jackson clenched his teeth. "Oww…"

The patient has suffered two deep distal puncture wounds on the right gastrocnemius with profuse bleeding." Dr. Baker set the leg down. "Does it hurt?"

"Y-y-eah." *Like burning white phosphorus.*

"Sorry." The doctor tapped the nurse's shoulder. "What's his blood pressure?"

The nurse pulled the stethoscope from her ears. "Ninety systolic by palpation. Heart rate is one-fifty and weak. Breaths are forty per minute, labored. Fluid buildup around his lungs."

Dr. Baker turned to the nurse behind him. "I don't need testing to know this man has a severe envenomation, not a dry bite. Call the lab. Tell them to mix six rounds anti-venom to stabilize his vital signs." He spoke to the nurse at his side. "Get him on oxygen via a positive pressure mask. Start IV fluids to boost his blood pressure before it gets too low."

Everyone moved in slow motion. The mask strap pulled his hair. He wanted to move it lower but couldn't. A nurse had hold of each arm, sticking catheters in his veins.

"Send a blood sample to the lab to check clotting factors. Insert a Foley."

Shit. Another tube up my penis.

"Get a urine sample to check renal function. Call for the portable x-ray to check for broken fangs in his calf and confirm fluid buildup in his lungs. Cut off his clothes. Put a pressure cuff on that leg to guard against compartment syndrome. If his blood pressure elevates exponentially, hypoxia could force us to amputate." Dr. Baker leaned into Jackson's face. "Can you still hear me, son?"

Jackson nodded. He couldn't speak with the mask pushing air down his throat.

"Good. We're giving you enough morphine to make the pain tolerable. I can't give you any more. You need to stay conscious. If you fall asleep, you might not wake up. Can the man with you make medical decisions on your behalf?"

Jackson pulled the mask from his face. "Yeah."

Dr. Baker pushed the mask down. "Don't do that again. You're already hypoxic." He turned to a nurse. "Give him two milligrams IV Lorazepam. Check his vitals every two minutes for the first twenty and every five thereafter. Start the anti-venom when it arrives. Note the time while I talk with his next of kin."

Poor Uncle Manny.

Mangus stood when Dr. Baker approached him with a chart in his hand. "How's Jackson?"

"Unstable, Mr. Malone. He's on pain medication for his comfort. Looks like the snake emptied all of its venom sac into his calf. I'll keep you apprised as the situation changes."

"Shit! Will he lose his leg?" Mangus wanted to barge into the treatment room. He couldn't let Jackson go through this with strangers. His logical side overrode his heart. He would only get in the way.

"Unknown. We'll have a better idea after four hours on the anti-venom."

"Can I see him?"

"No. We need to keep his vital signs under control. Seeing you so worked up could upset him." Dr. Baker opened the treatment room door and went inside.

Mangus sat in the chair and dropped his head into his hands. "I broke my promise to you, James. I'm sorry." He couldn't stop the tears or his imagination as James MacKenzie's ghostly image scowled at him from the wall.

April 2, 1985 – Harve, MT Hospital

Mangus stopped pacing in the waiting area when an orderly pushed Jackson on a gurney toward the elevator. His blanket-wrapped body was looped with lines and wires. An oxygen mask covered his face.

Dr. Baker approached Mangus. "I'm sending Jackson to the ICU. I need to tell you about the complications."

A cold shiver ran through him. "My son's going to die, isn't he?"

"I'm not sure. His organs started shutting down. It took twenty-two units of anti-venom to stabilize him. We have him on one-hundred percent oxygen and IV fluids. His blood work worries me. The clotting factors and platelet counts are low. We started six units of platelets to boost his levels. The next step is diuretics to reduce the fluid in his lungs and ice the leg to bring down the swelling."

"Do everything. I don't care what it costs." Mangus glanced at the payphone. *How do I tell Sara, Jackson may die? And Cathy. She's afraid of that bad news phone call. Now I have to make it.* "Send for a specialist if you have to." *I'll call the Navy, even if it puts Jackson in Leavenworth. At least he'll be alive. Then I can do everything in the open instead of slinking around for information.*

"We can take care of it, sir. Snakebites are common this time of year. The problem is the excess fluid buildup. If he can't pull enough oxygen into his lungs, he'll pass out. If he bumps that leg with it so swollen, it'll burst like an over-inflated balloon. If he gets cut, he'll bleed out because his blood won't clot."

Now I understand how Jackson feels. I want to crawl into a hole instead of calling Sara. "Then he stays until he can go home. Keep him sedated. Jackson pushes hard and gets out of bed too early."

"Yes, sir. We've given him medication to help with the pain. Our main focus now is keeping him conscious because his pulse is so weak."

"Good." *Now I have to call Sara and Cathy. Crap.*

Jackson raised his head when he heard Mangus' voice then dropped it back to the pillow. It was all he could do to breathe. Only the mask pushing oxygen into his lungs helped him remain among the living. He didn't want his godfather to spend any money on him. They had spent too much already. Thousands. Money the ranch needed for expenses, and this would cost them even more.

In spite of the medications, he was in pain. At most, it dampened the agony. Even his fingernails, toenails, and hair hurt. The muscle spasms were nearly unbearable, like rubber bands being pulled at both ends. His leg felt like it weighed a hundred pounds. His entire body shook. He went from freezing in a blast freezer to baking in an industrial oven. The seconds dragged by like hours.

Deep down, he knew that Dr. Baker made the right call by keeping him conscious, but this much suffering made him willing to roll the dice and take his chances by upping the morphine dose. His fifty-year-old body felt more like one-hundred.

Jackson closed his eyes. Time to find a place within himself without pain. Without heartbreak. Without sorrow. Somewhere before death became so much a part of his life.

CHAPTER 2

December 8, 1951
USMC Camp Pendleton, California

Jackson entered their house with a copy of his enlistment papers. He had just left the US Army recruiter's office in Oceanside. Since he was only seventeen, he hoped his mother would sign the permission form. But why wouldn't she? He'd worked his butt off to graduate a year early from high school for this purpose. She knew his plans, his dreams of going to West Point. This was the first stepping stone, enlisting during a time of war.

"Mom, I'm home," Jackson yelled in the entry hall.

"I'm in the kitchen, honey," his mother called.

Jackson went into the kitchen and watched his mother at the stove. He sniffed the air. She was cooking one of his favorite meals, pot roast with carrots, onions, and potatoes with green beans and corn. On the table, three place settings instead of two. Him, his mother…and maybe his older brother, Jim, in his first year at the Naval Academy.

"When's Jim getting home for winter break?"

His mother checked her watch. "Ten minutes. He called this morning to say his train would be late."

"Yeah, heard on the radio there were snowstorms in Maryland."

"Now…" His mother turned around. "Where have you been?"

Jackson held out the permission form. "Recruiter's office. Will you sign this for me, please?"

"Hmmm…so you went without me."

"Yes, ma'am. I wanted to get it done." He didn't want his mother going with him. No way did he want the recruiter thinking he was a mama's boy.

Mom took the paper and looked at it. Her expression didn't change. She wasn't happy with him. "So you chose infantry as a primary MOS? With the option to attend Airborne School?"

"Yes, I want to jump out of planes."

She tapped her finger on her lips. "Like your dad. James loves it too. I don't know, JJ, you just turned seventeen yesterday. Don't you want to wait and enjoy yourself for a few months? Be home for Christmas with your brother. You've done nothing but study and train at the gym."

Jackson wasn't sure she would sign it. "Mom…"

His mother's expression didn't change then she smiled. "Hand me a pen."

"Thanks." Jackson rummaged around in the kitchen junk drawer until he found a pen and gave it to her.

"When would you have to report for basic training?"

"The train leaves for Fort Benning on Tuesday…December 12th. I start basic on the 18th."

Before his mother could respond, someone knocked on the door.

"Wonder who that could be?" she said.

Jackson smiled. "Sergeant First Class Mason, my recruiter. I told him to give me thirty minutes then come by the house to get the form. That way, I can be on that train next week."

"Jackson Joseph MacKenzie, you are a brat…and I love you."

Jackson came to attention, chin tucked, back straight, hand cupped on the seams of his jeans. "Yes, ma'am."

"JJ…before you answer the door, I want you to think about something. With your dad in Korea, Jim at Annapolis, and you at basic, what would you think of me…seeing if the Army needs one more nurse? I can't sit in this house alone."

"Mom, that's up to you." Jackson hoped she wouldn't, but he understood why. Her father rode in the 7th Calvary in Indian Territory, Cuba, and the Philippines, and she adored him. Serving was in her blood.

December 18, 1951
Fort Benning, Georgia

Jackson stood in line at the barbershop with his gear and uniforms stuffed haphazardly in his duffle bag. Courtesy of his first trip to the quartermaster. His first few hours as a private had gone as expected. Lots of yelling, pushups, and a perpetual look of confusion on every recruit's face.

"Next," yelled the barber.

Jackson went in and sat in the chair. His hair was already in a Marine regulation high and tight like his father wore.

The barber buzzed the clippers, and what hair Jackson had fell to the floor.

"Next."

Jackson stood, grabbed his duffle bag, and joined the freshly shorn recruits in the hall.

The tedious intake process with its catalog of medical tests and paperwork, followed by a standing-room-only bus ride, pushed his patience to the limit. He hated being stuffed next to sweaty, stinky young

9

men who looked like deer in headlights. They reminded him of cattle on their way to slaughter.

"You there," someone called.

Jackson looked around as he got off the bus. "Yes."

A young man in civilian clothing came up to him. "You're doing it wrong."

"I'm doing what wrong?" Jackson asked. *Who is this jerk?*

"Standing at attention. You do it like this." The guy placed his hands next to his pockets. Not at all a correct form of attention. The knucklehead didn't have his feet at a forty-five-degree angle and his back was arched, not straight. Elbows bent. His shoulders were drooped. Not at all squared and his chin wasn't tucked in.

Who does he think he is? Jackson stared at the guy. *He acts like he already has three stripes. Moron.* Before he could correct him, the assistance drill sergeant, Sergeant McQueen, approached them. Jackson let the sergeant take care of the problem. You never want to gain the attention of anyone, but especially the drill sergeants on the first day.

"Private Wood!" Sergeant McQueen screamed.

Jackson knew that meant, *You're mine now, maggot!*

"Yes, sir," the man said.

"If you have so much time on your hands, how about you give us a show? Sing the *Star-Spangled Banner*! By yourself." Sergeant McQueen clenched his fists. His knuckles turned white. Sweat ran from under his garrison cap. His flashing eyes narrowed into crinkled dark slits.

"Huh?"

"Are you deaf? Do you need another medical exam for your hearing?"

"No, sir."

"Don't call me, sir, dipshit. I work for a living. And my parents aren't related," barked Sergeant McQueen. "Now sing!"

Wood stood straight and sang the *Star-Spangled Banner* in an off-key southern nasal twang.

Jackson withheld his laughter. The show-off got his just desserts.

A short time later, one hundred and fifty recruits tried to form straight lines, in alphabetical order, in under three minutes. Which equated to forty-five seconds in drill instructor time.

Jackson bit down on his impatience. He couldn't believe these men didn't know their lefts from their rights. Most of them tripped and fell over, dusting themselves off while the drill sergeants screamed at them to get moving. With the temperature hovering in the mid-fifties, cold sweat dripped down the back of his coat collar as he waited for the men to figure it out. His last name put him in the middle of the platoon.

Almost everyone failed the next test. Learning the names of total strangers, the men of his platoon. Knowing the drill, he rattled off the names of those around him correctly. Since this was a test that the recruits were meant to fail, he did pushups like the rest of 1st Platoon, Baker Company, 2nd Battalion, 19th Infantry Regiment.

The drill sergeants led them to the barracks. The wooden, two-story white building was old and reeked of mold. At the entrance, a rifle rack to lock up their M1 Garand .30-06 rifles when they were issued. Jackson thought that the air-cooled, gas-operated, clip-fed, semi-automatic, shoulder-fired weapon was cool. General George Patton had called it "the greatest battle implement ever devised."

His dad had taken him to the range at Pendleton many times and let him shoot one. The eight-round clip made a pinging sound when it ejected. He got to shoot the BAR-Browning Automatic Rifle once. Much too heavy. He'd rather stay with the M1 rifle or a carbine.

Both sides of the bay contained two bunks stacked on each other. Everyone went to their assigned bunk then placed their gear in their green wooden footlocker at the end. Each item had its place, rolled-up socks facing in the proper direction, underwear, handkerchiefs folded the Army way, comb, and razor. Behind each cot was a rack to hang clothing. The left sleeve always facing out. Above the rack, a shelf for a helmet. Throughout the room, nailed to the wooden support posts, two-pound red coffee cans half-filled with water. These were the "butt cans" for the smokers. But he didn't smoke, nor did he intend to start. Cigarette smoke always gave him a headache. Jackson was grateful he got the bottom bunk. He could scramble out of it faster. Ready for whatever the drill sergeants threw at him. From his father's stories, that was a given.

At 2000 hours, the senior drill sergeant, Sergeant First Class Nelson, gave them an hour of free time.

Jackson used it to get to know the men around him. "Hi, I'm Jackson MacKenzie." He held out his hand to the man on the bunk above him.

"Dale Webber," the young man, not any older than him, replied as he shook his hand. "Where are you from?"

"San Diego. You?"

"Fresno."

"So we're both from California," Jackson said.

"Looks that way. I guess we're battle buddies."

"Yeah, we go everywhere together." *If one of us gets caught alone, we're both in big trouble.*

They talked about a few things: school, girls, sports, movies. When Dale spoke about his parents, Jackson let him talk. He didn't want to give out any information about his mom or dad. Bringing up his father was a Marine colonel would only start more questions. Answers he didn't want to give. That would ultimately lead to someone figuring out he was the son of a Medal of Honor recipient, and he wanted to avoid that kind of scrutiny. He wanted to make it on his own, the only way he could do that: stay invisible. A fly on the wall absorbing information. That meant not making waves. He had to get along with everyone. You don't make friends by ordering your fellow recruits around or seeming too passive. The one thing he had to do was come off as a team player and let people like him.

Lights out—2100 hours. Jackson lay on his bunk, worn-out from the long day that started at 0500. At least he didn't draw fire watch on his first night. He stared at the bottom of the bunk above him. Occasional sobs drifted across the long expanse of the bay. He missed his mom and was a little homesick. Being a Marine brat, he understood one thing after going through his father's absence during WWII. After the oath, now he belonged to Uncle Sam.

Ninety-nine percent of surviving basic training was mental toughness. Take what the drill sergeants dished out and let it roll off your back. The only person who could defeat you was you. The other one percent, the drill sergeants. Their job, to break you down mentally and physically, then rebuild you into a living, breathing weapon, a United States Army soldier. Or, if you couldn't adapt to military life, they sent you packing with an Entry Level Separation.

March 19, 1952
Graduation Day – Fort Benning, GA

Four months of sweating, sleeplessness, long days, and even longer nights were over. His time in recruit hell had finally come to an end. Jackson was tired of the drill sergeant shenanigans, banging trashcan lids for wake-up and thousands of pushups.

Basic Training and Infantry School weren't hard, just hours of going through what his father already taught him. Shooting, combat tactics, leadership, close order drill, discipline, and military life. Learning how to kill and avoid being killed the Army way. Throwing grenades and sticking the bayonet on your M1 rifle into a cloth figure stuffed with straw on a swinging arm. He hated the crap jobs, assigned by the drill sergeants to make your life a never-ending purgatory. Kitchen police duty, peeling hundreds of potatoes, and scrubbing oversized pots and pans all weekend long.

Jackson stood at attention on the parade grounds wearing his service dress uniform with a light blue infantry cord hung over the right shoulder of his olive drab Ike jacket. He was proud to be a United States Army soldier. As an infantryman, he had entered a brotherhood within a brotherhood.

Only one thing marred the day. No one was there to watch him graduate. His father and mother were in Korea. So were Uncle Manny and Uncle Jason. Aunt Sara had to take care of the ranch. Aunt Janet was in charge of the Marine Corps Auxiliary at Pendleton. His older brother wanted to be at Jackson's graduation, but his brigade commander at the Naval Academy denied the request.

After he left for basic training, his mother reapplied to the Army, much to his chagrin. In need of surgical nurses, they accepted, promoted her, and shipped her off to war. Now she was the head nurse of the 8076th MASH unit.

Hundreds of spectators looked on. American and US Army flags flapped in the breeze. The band played John Philip Sousa marches as the two graduating companies marched in the pass in review.

Able and Baker companies lined up in front of the reviewing stand. The training cadre's commanding officer, Colonel Harlow, went down the steps and stood in front of them.

"Private MacKenzie, front and center," Colonel Harlow yelled.

Jackson stepped forward, squared his corner, went to the end of the formation, turned, and marched to the colonel. "Private MacKenzie reporting as ordered, sir!"

"Private MacKenzie, for your exemplary attitude and aptitude during training, you are being awarded Distinguished Honor Graduate for this training cycle. Congratulations, Private First Class MacKenzie."

"Yes, sir. Thank you, sir." Jackson accepted the PFC stripes and certificate in a black-bound case.

"Dismissed, PFC MacKenzie."

"Yes, sir." Jackson returned to his platoon with the stripes and certificate case clutched in his hand.

At the end of the ceremony, when dismissed by their company commander, the men rushed to the stands to meet their loved ones. Fathers, mothers, sisters, brothers, cousins, aunts, uncles, and children.

Jackson kept walking toward the barracks to sew on his chevron and pack everything in his duffle bag. Tomorrow he reported to his next assignment.

April 9, 1952
Airborne School Graduation - Fort Benning, GA

Jackson loved Airborne School. He didn't want it to end. Three weeks wasn't long enough. The adrenaline rush of freefall made him feel alive. One with his surroundings. Every time he leapt from a plane, he tingled as if on fire. The jerk of the risers and the floating made him feel on top of the world. Superman. Bulletproof. Unstoppable. Immortal.

Jackson stood with his company on the parade grounds. He wanted to get dismissed, go pack his gear, and use his pass for an evening on the town.

Colonel Thompson descended the steps and stood in front of them. "Private First Class MacKenzie, front and center," he yelled.

Again? Jackson left his spot in the formation and faced the colonel. "Private First Class MacKenzie reporting as ordered, sir."

"Private First Class MacKenzie, for your exemplary attitude and aptitude during training, you are being awarded Distinguished Honor Graduate for this training cycle. Congratulations, son.

"Yes, sir. Thank you, sir." Jackson accepted the certificate in a black-bound case.

"Dismissed, Private First Class MacKenzie."

"Yes, sir." Jackson returned his position.

"You are dismissed and good luck," Colonel Thompson yelled.

Hats flew in the air as applause came from the audience.

April 10, 1952

After breakfast at the leisurely hour of 0800, Jackson's platoon fell into formation in front of the company headquarters. It was zero hour. Their orders had been cut. They would find out their assignments. In a few minutes, everyone would receive his orders. That piece of paper would determine who would stay stateside and live and who would go to Korea and possibly die.

Jackson waited for his name to be called. Since it was alphabetical, it took several minutes.

Their company commander, Captain Hutchinson, pulled a page off his aide's clipboard. "Private First Class MacKenzie."

Jackson stepped forward, took the paper from him, and looked at it.

1st Cavalry Division

US Army, Japan/Korea

Replacement – Subject to TDY transfer to other commands within all US Army operations on the Korean peninsula. To remain attached to the 1st Cavalry Division upon completion of assignments in said other commands. Take the next available transport to Japan. Report to headquarters upon arrival.

Jackson was excited and disappointed at the same time. He wanted an assignment with the 101st or the 82nd Airborne and then go to Ranger School. But neither of those units were in Korea. The 1st Cavalry was currently in reserve in Japan after 549 days of continuous fighting and heavy losses. They could return to combat at any time. Now he was a straight leg again. *Crap.*

The TDY designation made him available to any unit needing a body. There were a lot of them. He might be assigned to the First Team but not likely to remain there for long. If he wound up in Korea, maybe he could finagle a pass to go see his mom and dad. That made this assignment better than Ranger School or Airborne. The Army did him a favor. Maybe. Hooah.

CHAPTER 3

April 14, 1952
Chitose Air Base, Hokkaidō, Japan

Jackson entered the outer office of the commanding general of the 1st Cavalry Division. The commanding officer of the headquarters company, Captain Granger, told him to report to the general and he had no idea why. Had he already done something wrong and didn't know it? Was he in trouble? A private normally didn't report to the division commander.

The one thing he did know, he was exhausted. It had been a long flight across the Pacific. Weather delays kept his plane grounded for hours in Guam. Sleeping on a C-124 Globemaster II with two hundred other men, all loaded down with an M1 rifle, pack, and duffle bag wasn't exactly comfortable. The cargo plane could hold tanks, field guns, bulldozers, and trucks, loaded through its clamshell forward doors, but today it felt way too small for that task. His neck was stiff and his back crunched when he walked from lying on the floor like a pretzel.

The first sergeant opened the door. "He's ready for you, Private."

Jackson marched into the office and came to attention. "Private First Class MacKenzie reporting as ordered, sir."

General Walker glanced up from his desk. "At ease, MacKenzie. Welcome to the 1st Cavalry Division."

Jackson snapped his arms behind his back. "Yes, sir."

"I'm sorry it won't be for long. You're going TDY to the 2nd Battalion, 27th Infantry Regiment, 25th Infantry Division."

"Yes, sir. I expected that to happen." *Interesting, the Tropic Lightning.*

"Good man." The general inspected him from head-to-toe. "I like what I see, MacKenzie. There's officer material in you." He picked up a folder from his desk. "This says you were the distinguished honor graduate for your basic and Airborne training classes. Top of your class twice is a hell of a feat for a seventeen-year-old."

"Yes, sir."

"Normally, this would happen at the regimental or battalion level...but after getting word of your achievements, I decided to do this." General Walker pulled two pieces of cloth from the folder. "These are yours."

Jackson looked at what the general handed him. "Corporal stripes, sir?"

"Yes. You earned them through your exemplary aptitude and attitude during training. You're an assistant squad leader now for the 25th, Corporal MacKenzie. Report to my clerk for your transfer orders."

Jackson snapped to attention. "Yes, sir."

"Corporal MacKenzie."

"Yes, sir."

"Stay alive. I want you back."

"I'll sure try, sir."

"Dismissed."

Jackson turned on his heel and left the room. He ran to the transitory barracks and hand-sewed the stripes on his shirt. Then he packed his duffle bag. His orders said to report to the airfield at 1900 for a flight to Korea. Just what his back needed. Another flight on a bumpy cargo plane.

April 21, 1952
Main camp of the 25th Infantry Division

Jackson released his squad from formation as his sergeant looked over his shoulder, observing him. His men did well today at the range. Every man scored one hundred percent. He had good men under his command. Trained, disciplined, and smart.

One thing had all of them at a disadvantage. Youth and inexperience. They were all replacements seventeen to eighteen years old with no combat under their belts and fresh from infantry training in the states. He hoped no one would crack under the pressure of combat, including himself. It was one thing to talk big in front of others but another to back it up under fire.

Sergeant Gonzales gripped his shoulder as the men disappeared into the barracks. "Excellent job. You're a natural leader, MacKenzie. I'm going to recommend you for NCO Command School. Who knows when you can go, but I need to get you on the list."

"Thanks, Sarge."

"Go grab a shower and get some chow."

"Yes, Sergeant. Do you mind if I go see the LT first?"

"Of course not. Go. Knucklehead."

Jackson nodded and went to his platoon commander's office at 2nd Battalion headquarters. He came to attention in front of the desk. "Can I speak with you, Lieutenant Wheeler?"

Second Lieutenant Wheeler, who, at twenty-three, was only six years older, nodded. "Sure, Corporal. At ease. What do you need?"

Jackson placed his arms behind his back. "A one-day pass, sir."

"Where are you going?"

"First Marine Division headquarters, sir."

"Why would you want to visit jarheads?"

Jackson ground his teeth together to hold in his temper. "My father's the commanding officer of the 1st Marine Regiment. I haven't seen him since he deployed to Korea."

Lt. Wheeler pulled out a piece of paper. "Marine brat, huh?"

"Yes, sir."

"At least you had the common sense to join the Army. I like the idea of a corporal from the 25th Infantry walking into the den of the 1st Marines and saluting its commanding officer. As a West Point grad, I'll take revenge on Navy any way I can." Wheeler signed a form. "Request approved." He handed the paper to him. "Have fun."

Jackson didn't care why his commanding officer gave him the pass. He was happy to have received it. "Yes, sir."

"Dismissed."

Jackson went to his quarters and readied his service dress uniform. He brushed the lint off his olive drab pants and Ike jacket with the 1st Cavalry Division patch on the left shoulder. Even in the 25th Infantry, he was still assigned to the 1st Cav. This assignment was only temporary. The last item on his list, polish his brown dress shoes until he could see his reflection in the leather.

April 22, 1952 – 0600 hours

Jackson climbed out of his bunk at reveille. He showered, shaved, and put on his service dress uniform. Crunched for time, breakfast was a can of peaches, peanut butter, and crackers he traded for the cigarettes in one of his C-rations. Slowly, he slipped his garrison cap over his regulation high and tight, exactly like his father wore, making sure the cap sat at the correct angle. After checking his appearance in the bathroom mirror, he buttoned his coat. He straightened the light blue infantry cord on his right shoulder, so it hung perfectly. To make sure his expert marksmanship badge with the rifle, carbine, and pistol bars was secure, he gave it a small tug. *Don't want it falling off. Shot perfect scores, thanks to dad's training.*

Before he left the barracks, he ran a cloth over the Airborne wings above his left breast pocket to make them sparkle. He cleaned the dust off his dress shoes with the same cloth. His father would inspect him at first sight. Everything had to be perfect before he arrived.

Jackson checked his appearance in the jeep mirror. He climbed into the driver's side and headed for the main gate.

The MP stepped out from the guard shack. "Pass."

"Here you go, Sergeant." Jackson held out the piece of paper.

The MP glanced at the paper and raised the crossbar.

Jackson drove toward the 1st Marine Division headquarters. Since it was only thirty minutes away, he had plenty of time. He wanted to see his mother too, but her unit was several hours away by jeep. His pass had a report time. 2100 hours. When he got back, he would apply for a weekend pass to visit her. The most important thing today, saluting his dad for the first time as a soldier.

With no enemy activity in the area, the drive went smoothly. The only thing Jackson passed, donkey carts laden with freight, and other military vehicles. He pulled up to the 1st Marine Division gate then held out his Armed Forces of the United States/ U.S. Army ID card and one-day pass.

The staff sergeant snatched the papers from Jackson's hand. "What does a grunt want on our base? Unless it's to clean the head."

Jackson glared at him. "What's your unit, Sergeant?"

"First Marines, of course."

"Don't you recognize the name?" *That should get a reaction.*

The man rechecked Jackson's ID card. "MacKenzie? As in Colonel MacKenzie?"

"Yes, he's my father. I suggest you raise the crossbar. I've heard some of his butt chewings. Don't you dare call him. I may be wearing an Army uniform, but I still bite," Jackson growled.

"I bet, if you're his son." The sergeant raised the crossbar. "Proceed up the road. Take the left fork to headquarters."

"Where does the right take you?"

"Motor pool."

Jackson parked at the motor pool. He walked across the compound toward headquarters. As he got closer, he changed direction and came up behind two men with their backs to him. Five feet away, he stopped. "Corporal MacKenzie reporting as ordered, sir!"

Colonel James MacKenzie spun around as did Major General Mangus Malone.

Jackson stood tall at perfect attention. He rendered a textbook salute. The way his father taught him.

Dad and Uncle Manny returned the salute. They dropped their hands together.

Jackson did the same but remained at attention with his thumbs on the seams of his trousers. He saw several enlisted Marines headed their way out of his peripheral vision but didn't move.

The first to arrive, Technical Sergeant Nichols. Uncle Jason. He smiled, turned, and ran off the other Marines.

Dad and Uncle Manny walked around him.

"What do you think, Colonel?" Mangus said.

"Not bad." Dad tugged on the back of Jackson's jacket. "Still has the new smell."

They stopped in front of him.

"At ease, Corporal MacKenzie," said Mangus.

Jackson spread his feet, shoulder-width apart, and put his arms behind his back. He maintained eye contact with the general as the ranking officer present. "Yes, sir."

Dad broke military protocol. He grabbed him in an all-encompassing bear hug, which Jackson returned exuberantly. They remained in the position for a long time.

Jackson stepped back when his father released him and straightened his jacket.

"You already made corporal?" Dad pointed at Jackson's sleeve. "How'd you manage that, son?"

Jackson puffed out his chest with his back ramrod straight. "Distinguished honor graduate for my basic training class and Airborne School, sir. The brass thought I was ready for it. At least that's how General Walker explained it to me. I'm an assistant squad leader now." *Need to explain the 1st Cav patch.* "I'm TDY with the 25th Infantry Division."

"Top of your class for basic and Airborne School, a corporal, and assistant squad leader. I'm proud of you, Jackson. You sure worked your butt off, but you're a MacKenzie, so it's expected." Dad's voice echoed across the square.

Jackson snapped to attention. "Yes, sir."

Mangus crossed his arms. "I expect the best out of you as well. I'd rather see you in a Marine uniform, but you joined on your own instead of being drafted. I will see you at West Point or Annapolis next year. Even if I have to push your appointment through Congress…in person."

"General Malone, I want to make it myself. You know that's why I enlisted instead of taking the easy road by using the automatic appointment from Dad's Medal of Honor. I'll get a recommendation to the academy on my own merit."

"Just what I'd expect from a MacKenzie."

Uncle Jason marched up and snapped to attention. "Can I have a go at inspecting our new recruit, sir?"

Mangus waved at Jackson. "Have at it, Sergeant."

Jason walked around Jackson and stopped in front of him. "Your uniform looks perfect, Corporal MacKenzie. More than I would expect from Army training. You should've been a leatherneck like your dad. I heard him say you were the distinguished honor graduate for boot camp, then Airborne School, and assistant squad leader. I'd expect nothing less from you, young man."

Jackson came to attention. "Yes, Sergeant Nichols," he boomed out in his loudest voice.

Jason shook his head. "You have the rest of these young Marines wondering who you are to get saluted then hugged by the colonel. Since you two are mirror images of each other, it should be obvious, right, Corporal MacKenzie?"

"Yes, Sergeant Nichols."

Dad took command. "How long can you stay?"

Jackson handed over the one-day pass. "I have to be back at camp by 2100 hours, sir."

Dad stuffed the pass into Jackson's breast pocket. "Son, you're on my base. Drop the sir and colonel crap. You're only seventeen. Call me Dad. Let me take you around and show you off as my son. You will eat dinner with me, young man. Don't worry. I'll make sure you're back on time. If something comes up, I'll get you an extension. I want to spend some time with you. Neither of us knows when we might get another chance while we're in Korea with a war going on."

"Yes sir...errr...I mean, Dad."

Mangus winked. "You'd better keep it straight, or you'll pay like a Marine if you get it wrong."

"Yes, sir, General Malone." Jackson realized his mistake again. "Errrr...I mean, Uncle Manny."

"See, even Army guys can learn sometimes," Mangus said. "Right, Sergeant Nichols?"

"Yes, sir." Jason smiled at Jackson's small but rectified mistake. "It seems they can."

Mangus patted Jackson's shoulder. "I'm glad you're here. James has been talking about you all week. It's nice to see you salute him for real like you did as a little boy. See you both later. I'll be in my office." He marched smartly toward headquarters.

Jason gripped Jackson's shoulder. "Me too, kid. I'm proud of you. You're pig-headed and stubborn like your dad and independent like your mom. The perfect MacKenzie. Too special to wear Army green. You'll go far in the ranks of the Army and even farther if you joined the Corps. Good luck with obtaining your appointment. It shows a lot about your character. I have to attend to my duties. See you later." He left in the direction of the barracks.

Dad took him to the rifle range first. They watched the men go through marksmanship practice. The roar of M1 rifles and the ping of ejecting clips filled the air then stopped as the men reloaded and changed positions.

A staff sergeant walked up. "Who's the grunt, Colonel?"

Dad jumped into the man's face. "My son, knucklehead. Got a problem with it? He's more squared away than you and most of the men on the base. Tuck in your shirt."

Jackson cringed as the sergeant scurried away, stuffing the tail of his shirt into his pants. "Dad, it's okay. I am a grunt."

"No, it's not. You're with me. It was disrespectful to both of us. It'll get around. No one will make the same mistake." Dad pointed at headquarters. "I have an idea. Follow me." In the main office, Dad stopped at the desk. "Where's the regimental photographer?"

A technical sergeant came out of an office. "Here, sir. Need something?"

"Grab your camera, Sergeant Drummond. I want pictures with my son."

"Yes, sir." Drummond left then returned with a black Kodak camera. He posed them in front of the Marine Corps flag with the campaign streamers of the 1st Marines and the American flag.

For the first picture, Jackson stood at his dad's right side, shoulders squared, chin tucked in, and chest out. In the second picture, he faced his dad and saluted him. The third, they sat in chairs with the flags in the background.

Dad stood and patted Jackson's shoulder. "I'll send you copies after they're developed. Expect a package in next week's mail delivery."

"Yes, sir."

"Jackson, think about your answer."

Oops. "Yes, Dad."

"Better."

Jackson was uncomfortable. He felt like a heel after witnessing the dressing down at the range. It took effort to force himself to relax and enjoy the time with his father.

"Want to see the pack horses?"

"You have horses?"

"Yes, you crazy kid." Dad led him to the corral where the 1st Marine Division kept its horses.

Jackson climbed over the fence and waded into the herd. One, in particular, took to him. She shoved her head into his chest and followed him around like a dog. A small chestnut mare with a white blaze and three socks. He grabbed her halter to read the brass nameplate. "Hi, Reckless. Wish I had some peppermints." *I'd love to take you back to the base with me. Don't know where I'd hide you and Dad might get mad at me.*

Dad leaned over the wooden fence. "Jackson, let's go. That's an order."

"Gotta go, girl. Keep your head down." Jackson petted her blaze. He jumped over the fence then wiped his hands on his pants. "Ready, Dad."

"Time to check in with my staff. Come with me." Dad marched to headquarters and went inside.

Jackson stood two feet behind and to the right.

Dad turned at the waist. "Get your butt up here." He pointed at his right side.

"Yes, Dad." Jackson took a step forward to stand next to his father.

Major Daniels held out his hand. "Congratulations. Good luck in continuing the family tradition. I heard about what you've accomplished from Sergeant Nichols."

"Thank you, sir. How's Amy?"

"About to start college. She said you took her to the prom."

"Yes, sir. She turned Jim down."

"Bet he didn't like that."

"No, sir. He sulked for two days."

Several officers approached to congratulate him. Jackson talked to each one and shook their hands. He knew all of them. They came by the house on occasion to speak with his father.

After a nice dinner at the officer's table, an hour of coffee, and talking about the war, 2000 hours rolled around.

Jackson stood. "Time for me to go, Dad."

"Let me walk you to your jeep." Dad pushed back his chair.

They walked side by side to the motor pool.

"That's mine." Jackson pointed at the green jeep with US Army stenciled on the hood.

Dad grabbed him in a bear hug and held on tightly.

Jackson wiggled his way out of his father's grasp. "Dad, I do need to breathe."

"Sorry, son." Dad straightened his shirt." I miss you and your brother. You're the youngest and so much more like me than Jim." He brushed a tear away with his hand. "Keep your head down. The last thing I want is to tell your mother you got hurt or even worse, killed in action. Do your duty like the honorable man you are and I expect you to be. I love you so much."

"I love you too. Take your own advice. I'll apply for another pass when I get some leave time. We're heading to the front in a couple of days. I don't know when that might be." Jackson wiped a tear from his cheek. "Keep Uncle Manny and Uncle Jason out of the line of fire."

Dad chuckled. "I will. They'll appreciate the fact you cared enough to say it. Nothing's changed with you. Kim was always on your butt about not using a handkerchief. You dirtied so many suit jackets with snot. I can't say this enough. I love you. Be careful."

Jackson didn't want to leave, but he had to get back to his base. He came to attention and gave his dad his best salute.

Dad did the same and dropped his hand.

Jackson climbed into his jeep and started it. Before he could put the vehicle in gear, his father did something unexpected. He removed Jackson's garrison cap, ruffled his hair, kissed him on the forehead then replaced the cap.

Speechless and embarrassed, Jackson stuck out his hand. His dad took it in a tight grip. He didn't think his dad would ever let go.

"Keep yourself safe, squirt." Dad dropped his hand.

"I'll do my best." Jackson put the jeep in gear and drove away. He checked the rearview mirror. His father was standing in the road waving goodbye.

CHAPTER 4

June 25, 1952 – 1600 hours

Jackson returned to base with his patrol. He and his men were bone-tired, muddy, and ready for some time off after five days in the field near the Mundung-ni Valley. He could see Heartbreak Ridge in the distance. All he really wanted right now, a shower and a hot meal. The crappy C-rations turned old after day one.

Things in the 27th Infantry Regiment had been slow. Their job—patrol and maintain the defensive positions around the 38th parallel. Even though they had been in a few skirmishes with the North Koreans and Chinese, it hadn't amounted to much. Other than a few minor wounds, his squad was the same and ready to fight.

As Jackson sat on his bunk, one of the new transfers into the platoon came into the barracks. He knew the guy by sight but not the private's name.

The man came up to him and nodded. "Corporal."

"Yes. What can I do for you?"

"Lieutenant Wheeler approved your request to call the 8076th MASH. The call will go through at 1800 hours. He also said that at this time, he can't swing a weekend pass for you."

Shit. Can't go see Dad or Mom. I'll try again next month. "Thanks." That gave him two hours to shower and grab a bite to eat at the mess hall.

"Who are you calling, Corporal, if I may ask?"

Jackson smiled. "My mother. She's the head nurse at the 8076th."

"Oh." The private turned and left.

Wonder what that meant. Jackson took off his mud-covered shirt then grabbed his shaving kit, towel, and fresh clothes. He went to the shower whistling a happy tune. Finally, he could hear his mother's sweet, angelic voice. Today, he wanted to hear her say, *Jackson Joseph MacKenzie.*

At 1800 hours, Jackson put the handset of the field telephone the company clerk handed him to his ear. He listened to static. Time slowed as he waited. It seemed like years until another voice came on the line. Slightly off, tinny, but the voice embedded in his memory. His mother.

"Jackson, is that you?"

Jackson smiled. "Yeah, Mom…I mean Major MacKenzie."

"Don't you major me, Jackson Joseph MacKenzie."

He got what he wanted. "Okay, Mom."

25

"James told me that you visited him."

"Yeah, right after I got here. Haven't been able to secure another pass. Sorry, Mom. I wish I could see you."

"Same here, son. Just do your duty, keep your head down and go home. I'm supposed to rotate back to the states next month. I'll have your favorite meal waiting for you when you get home."

Jackson's mouth watered thinking about his mom's pot roast, potatoes, green beans, corn, and a vanilla milkshake for dessert. "Can't wait to get home and see you, Dad, and Jim. Take care of yourself, please."

"I'm not the one near the lines. You and James are the ones who are in danger. Promise me to keep your head on a swivel. Stay frosty, son."

Jackson heard the concern in her voice. He was still her baby. "I will, Mom. Listen to your own advice. The gooks bomb hospitals too."

"Yeah, we've had to bug out a couple of times. Nothing got close. Just take care of yourself, squirt."

Jackson ducked his head. If any of his buddies heard that nickname, he would never hear the end of it. "I will, Mom. I'll see you in a few months."

"I'll send you underwear and cookies for Christmas. I'm sure Sara will send stuff too."

"Tell her chocolate chip, sugar cookies, candy bars, and…toilet paper. The stuff here is sandpaper. It rubs your butt raw."

"Your dad said the same thing. You two are so much alike. Count on it. I love you."

"I love you too, Mom." The phone clicked. Jackson waited to see if her wonderful voice returned. Nothing but static. He placed the handset in the box. "Thanks, Miller."

"No problem. Glad to help. The LT said you've earned it. You playing poker with us tonight?"

Jackson shook his head. "Nah. I'm going to bed early after I finish my book."

"You and your books. Pass that one to me when you finish it."

"Sure." Jackson placed his cap on his head and left headquarters.

June 26, 1952 – 0600 hours

Jackson scraped the nasty powdered eggs into the trash bin and placed his plate in the bucket next to the wall. The toast and oatmeal drenched in butter and brown sugar ranked as the only things halfway edible. He wished the mess cooks could make Marine coffee, not the watered-down crap in the pot. It tasted like used coffee grounds filtered through a dirty, sweaty t-shirt. Horrible.

Sergeant Gonzalez ran into the mess hall, paused for a second, then doubled-timed over to him. "Come with me to headquarters!"

"What's wrong?" Jackson asked.

"The Chinese are trying to take Old Baldy again. We've been ordered to help reinforce Hill 266."

"Isn't that out of our operating area? That's under the 45th."

"True, so General Gatlin just attached our company to the 180th Infantry to help out."

Jackson's heart climbed into his throat as he ran with Gonzalez to headquarters.

After the briefing, he grabbed his pack, M1 rifle, holstered .45 Colt pistol, gas mask, web belt, Mark I trench knife, and ten bandoleers of .30-06 ammo from his locker. The WW I trench knife, called the "knuckle buster," was a gift from his father, sent with the pictures of their day together at the 1st Marine Division camp. It came with a note. "This might come in handy. Love Dad." Jackson ran to the deuce-and-a-half parked on the road and climbed in the back with his squad.

Today, he would learn if he was a soldier or a big talker.

No guts, no glory.

The truck dropped them off near Hill 266. They joined Captain Tiller and the 180th Infantry in the trenches. The sticky black mud stank of mildew, death, old pee, and shit. Mortars and heavy machine-gun fire rained down upon them, making it hard to move over the crest of the hill. Unable to gain headway, the men regrouped. Fox Company took over holding the left and right fingers of Old Baldy. Charlie Company gained control of old Outpost 11. Able Company went around to the right to flank the enemy defenders.

Lt. Wheeler led his platoon to the left flank to pin the Chinese between them. Within minutes, the mortar fire raining down on them thickened like fog. Unable to move forward, the platoon piled into the trenches for protection. Machine-gun fire from the ridge mowed down Lt. Wheeler and First Sergeant Porter. They dropped dead in their tracks, their bodies nothing but swiss-cheesed hamburger.

Jackson looked around. Next to him, Sgt. Gonzalez lay with a hole in his helmet. Whitish-gray brain matter and blood dribbled down his face. Those still among the living were young men, mostly privates with wide eyes, ducking behind the trench walls. No one fired back, their rifles held in quivering hands or lying in the mud.

The *medic, medic* calls, close and far away, overlapped each other. Screams of the wounded sounded over the thunder of shells and the rat-a-tat of machine-gun fire.

Jackson took a deep breath, trying to slow his racing heart. Only then did he realize how fast and heavy he was breathing, how tense his muscles were under his uniform. Rock hard, making it hard to move at first. Sweat rolled from under his helmet into his eyes. Butterflies rolled around in his stomach, but he wasn't scared. Nervous. Anxious. Angry that his friends were dying. His senses went into overdrive. He smelled the iron of blood in the air. The stink of gunpowder. Heard the roar of gunfire. Felt the pressure in his chest from the explosions.

Clutch time. Jackson ran at a low crouch, back and forth, along the trench, issuing orders. "Find a target and start firing. Don't waste ammo. One shot, one kill." He stopped next to Private First Class Kyle Pagano. "You okay, Kyle?"

Kyle nodded. "Yeah, think so."

"Take your squad and go reinforce our right flank. We don't want the gooks climbing up our six."

"Got it." Kyle grabbed the six men next to him. "You heard him, let's go." The men ran off, disappearing in the thickening black smoke.

Jackson shifted over to PFC Miller. He still had his BAR-Browning Automatic Rifle. "Set that up. You have all the long-range shots. No one gets close."

Miller took a breath, heaved the BAR over the edge of the trench, and flipped out the bipod. The private with him started handing him full magazines from the ammo box at his feet.

Jackson pointed at the three men next to him. "Potter, you, Malloy, and Woolen have the left flank. If you let anyone through, we're all going home in a box."

Potter's eyes widened. He fidgeted on his feet. Jackson could tell he was trying to rake in his courage. "Hey, I'm scared too. We need to protect our wounded buddies."

"Y-y-yes, sir." Potter and the other two men crawled off to the left. The smoke obscured them quickly.

Jackson grabbed the handset off the pack of the radioman next to him. He had no idea the call signs of the 180th Infantry or the 45th. "Screw it." Right now, he didn't care about correct comm traffic and pushed the talk button. "This is Pied Piper. Anyone copy?"

"Pied Piper, is this actual?"

"No, the LT is dead. So is the first sergeant."

"Who's in command?"

Jackson paused. "I am, sir. Corporal MacKenzie."

"What's your sit-rep?"

"Maintaining our position at the moment. Covering Charlie and Fox Company's left flank. Low on ammo. One BAR still operational, small arms, and a few grenades. Need medical help and reinforcements."

"Can't reinforce you or get medical help to your location. The Chinese have mined the roads. Hold out until morning."

Morning? "Sir, half the platoon is dead or dying."

"Do your best, MacKenzie, but that location is vital to maintaining possession of Old Baldy. Out."

"Shit!" *Follow my training. Pay attention to everything. Don't let my guard down. Just act, don't think. Improvise. I can be scared later…if I live through this.*

Thick smoke covered the area like a blanket. Jackson tied a cloth around his nose and mouth to filter it out. He placed his M1 rifle with the bayonet attached on the edge of the trench and laid his Mark 1 trench knife next to it. The handguard, fashioned like brass knuckles, would be great for bashing heads. It gave him the ability to strike, stab, and slash in close quarters. They might have to go hand-to-hand if the gooks got close. The Chinese were known for making human wave attacks to overrun positions. And he had his orders. Maintain this position at all costs.

Shells rained down like a thunderstorm. Screams filled the air from the wounded and the dying. Fire lit the night sky. Explosions rocked the ground in an unrelenting earthquake.

Jackson turned as someone ran toward him. He aimed his rifle into the smoke then recognized the face in the haze and lowered the muzzle. "Hey, Kyle. How's it on your end?"

"Good. You've got everyone set up perfectly. Here?"

"We're tight for the moment."

A flash lit up a distant hillock followed by the sound of a ricochet.

Jackson felt something slam into his chest. The heavy impact took his breath away. Burning pain erupted on his left side, up through his neck, down his arm and shoulder. The agony went through him with each beat of his heart.

Kyle helped him sit in the mud. "You've been shot."

"Yeah, pack it with your pressure bandage. We don't have anything else." *Mom and Dad are going to be so mad at me.* His ears would be a lot smaller after they got done with him. Practically chewed off.

"Okay." Kyle wound the bandage around Jackson's chest outside his fatigues. Not a lot of blood, which was a good thing.

Jackson sat there for a few minutes. The pain faded. Still there, but that fight or flight adrenaline kicked in. At least he could function. He held out his hand. "Help me up."

Kyle pulled him to his feet. "You sure?"

"Yeah. These guys are more important than me. Go back to your position, Kyle. Thanks."

Kyle nodded. "I want to see you alive when the sun comes up."

Jackson held onto his side, over the bandage. "Me too."

The hours dragged on. Occasionally a flare glowed red in the night sky, showing the muddy slope in front of them. Finally, an orange tint lit the eastern horizon. Then the sun appeared.

Jackson had no idea of the passage of time as he stared over his M1 sights. He was lightheaded from fatigue and blood loss. Slowly, he shook his head to stay awake.

Behind them came the sound of men advancing. Heavy running footsteps in the mud. He sure hoped the Chinese hadn't broken through the lines and gotten behind them.

The private ten feet to his right turned. "Corporal, reinforcements made it."

Jackson pushed himself to a standing position as men jumped into the trench.

A young man wearing a single silver bar on his collars approached him. "Are you MacKenzie?"

"Yes, sir."

"Report."

"Lieutenant Wheeler and First Sergeant Porter died immediately, sir. So did most of the sergeants. I took over and set up what's left of the platoon as you see them now. We maintained our position as ordered, sir." Jackson couldn't remain on his feet. He sat hard in the mud. His vision blurred, then everything went dark and took the pain away.

June 28, 1952 – 8055th MASH

Someone lightly slapped his cheeks. "Corporal MacKenzie, can you open your eyes for me?" a young female voice asked.

Jackson opened his eyes to bright lights. Sunlight through the windows. Glaring lamps overhead. They gave him a headache. He slammed his eyes shut.

Someone shook his shoulder. "Please open your eyes."

Jackson forced them open. *Must be a field hospital.* The ward was an open bay, cots lined up on both sides separated by curtain partitions and filled with wounded men. A MASH unit. He looked around. Nurses and one white-coated doctor moved around the room. Maybe this was his mother's unit. The 8076th. "Where am I?" he whispered.

The young lieutenant smiled. "The 8055th MASH."

Not Mom's. I need to get word to her. "Could you do me a favor?"

"What, Corporal?"

"Contact Major MacKenzie at the 8076th MASH. Tell her I'm here."

"Do you know the major?"

"Yes. She's my mother."

The lieutenant smiled. "Sure." She adjusted the drip on his IV line. "You need to stay still. That bullet passed within inches of your heart, missed your lung, and lodged under your shoulder blade. You're a lucky young man. It only did extensive soft tissue damage to your shoulder, pectoral and trapezius muscles."

Behind her, a large bear of a man in green fatigues entered the ward.

Jackson recognized him immediately. Major General Mangus Malone, the commanding officer of the 1st Marine Division. His godfather. He couldn't read a specific emotion on Uncle Manny's face. Lips in a straight line. Jaw clenched. Eyes narrowed and bloodshot. Cheeks bright red and shiny. Not anger...sorrow, remorse, heartache, regret, sadness, pain.

Mangus sat in the chair next to the bed. He didn't say a word. Instead, he grabbed Jackson's hand and dropped a set of dog tags on a ball chain into his open palm.

Jackson looked at the tags then at Mangus. He could barely make out the name on them under the dried blood. MacKenzie. His godfather was there, not his dad. "No...no...no..."

"I'm so sorry, kid." Tears fell from Mangus' eyes.

Jackson closed his hand tightly around the dog tags. They sliced deep into his palm. He didn't care. His dad was gone. Blood dripped between his fingers.

His nurse tried to pry his hand open. He refused. That pain he wanted to feel, needed to feel. It hurt all the way to his soul.

"Corporal, open your hand. I need to treat that cut," she said.

"No!" Jackson jerked his arm away from her. "Leave me alone."

Mangus grabbed her arm. "Do it later. Please. Let him grieve."

The nurse looked confused. "Grieve? For who?"

"Those dog tags belonged to his father, Colonel James MacKenzie, Marine Corps. He was killed yesterday."

"Oh no. He asked me to contact his mother at the 8076th. Does she know?"

"Not yet. Haven't been able to contact her. I sent a messenger. It was more important to tell Jackson first."

The nurse went to the other side of the room and spoke with the doctor on duty.

Jackson looked up into his godfather's eyes. "What happened?"

"Sniper in a tree on the other side of the fence. Your dad saw the glint of the rifle scope. He shoved Sergeant Nichols and me down then jumped on top of us. The round hit him in the back and lodged in his lung. He died in my arms. His last wish was for me to watch over you, and I will. I can't ignore a blood promise."

"Don't worry about me, Uncle Manny. You need to tell Mom."

"She's my next stop. You going to be okay?"

"Yeah...eventually."

Mangus laid several pictures on the end table. "I found the top one in your dad's pocket. The others were in his wallet. "I'll see you later, kid. Do what the doctors tell you to." He ruffled Jackson's hair and left the ward. The doctor followed him outside.

Jackson picked up the pictures. The first one was him and his father saluting each other. The others were of them sitting in chairs and side by side in front of the Marine Corps flag with campaign streamers and the American flag. The pictures taken at the 1st Marine Division base in April. He placed them against his chest with the dog tags and cried. He didn't care who watched. Who saw him. His father was dead. Gone forever. Anyone watching could go to hell.

June 29, 1952

Jackson awoke the next morning. Instead of his nurse hovering over him, Uncle Manny sat next to the bed. His eyes were puffy and bloodshot as if he had been crying all night. Dried tears streaked his face, and his cheeks were rosy red with broken blood vessels underneath.

On the other side of the ward, the nurses and one doctor were crying. Outright bawling with sniffs, sobs, and wails.

Mangus' expression was sad, his lips drawn tightly and face contorted. He sat motionless, slouching in the chair, unlike the normal, squared away Marine.

Jackson looked at the medical staff then at Mangus. What would make them cry? *No. Mom?* He held out his hand.

Mangus dropped a set of dog tags into his palm. These were blackened and bent. But the name was readable. MacKenzie, Kimberly A. "Her jeep ran over a land mine coming back from an aid station two days ago. The explosion killed her and her driver instantly. The chaplain told me that a closed casket service is recommended because…it ripped her to pieces. The mortuary service hopes they found everything. Much of it was…unrecognizable. I'm so sorry, Jackson."

He couldn't help himself. Jackson let the tears fall. His mother. His angel. His support when things got tough during WWII. The woman who held him when he was scared, sick, hurt, and lonely, missing his dad, was gone.

"Let it out, son. It doesn't make you any less of a man." Mangus tried to smile and failed miserably. He wiped tears from his cheek with his hand.

Another man crossed the ward. On one collar, a gold oak leaf, the other, the insignia of the medical corps. A caduceus—the staff of Hermes, two snakes winding around a winged staff. He stopped behind Mangus. "You need to suck it up, Corporal. You're a man. A soldier. Or are you a sobbing little baby? Not worthy of wearing an Army uniform. You cried yesterday too."

Mangus stood so fast, his chair went flying backward. It bounced off the man's leg. Mangus spun, grabbed the man's shirt, then turned and shoved him against the wall. The major's feet dangled, not touching the floor. "What do you see on my collar, asshole?"

The major's eyes went wide. A wet spot spread across his groin. "Two stars," he whispered.

"You got that right. You just disrespected my godson and his parents. You will apologize to him. Do I make myself perfectly clear?"

"Y-y-yes, sir."

Jackson tried to concentrate. His vision was blurring. A warm feeling ran through him. He looked over. The nurse was injecting something into his IV line.

The major leaned over the bed. "I'm…"

Everything went black.

July 2, 1952
121st Medical Evacuation Hospital – Seoul, South Korea

Jackson sat up in his bed when his godfather entered the room. He adjusted the sling strap supporting his injured left shoulder. "Hi…Uncle Manny. Sorry I went to sleep on you at the MASH unit."

"Hey, kid. Don't worry about it. I saw what the nurse was doing." Mangus straightened the jacket of his green Marine Corps Service A uniform and sat in the chair next to the bed. "Then your doctor read me the riot act for not warning him. He stuck his foot so far up my ass it came out of my mouth. And I took it quietly because he was right. How are you doing?"

"Okay, I guess. My shoulder hurts but my heart hurts more."

Mangus' eyes widened. "The doctor said it wasn't hit. Just soft tissue damage to your shoulder."

"No, no, no…" Jackson tapped his chest. "In here."

"Ignore me. I'm dense today…a downright babbling moron."

"You're entitled, Uncle Manny. Does Jim know?"

Mangus took a deep breath. "Yes. The Casualty Assistance officer informed him yesterday. I called him as well and told him about you. He's getting a week's emergency leave from summer training for the funeral."

"Poor Jim. Take care of him for me."

"I will. I've only got a few more minutes. I'm escorting your mom and dad home on the transport in a couple of hours. I trusted no one else with the duty and…James was my best friend."

Jackson sniffed. "Yeah. Not too many generals escort bodies home. They'd be honored. I wish the docs would let me go stateside with you for the funeral. They don't want me moved for a few more days. I'll do my rehab here and go back to my unit."

"I know. I talked to your doctor before I came in. Speaking of that, I read the after-action report submitted by Captain Tiller. He was impressed by your leadership and tactics. Says you combined a partial pincer movement with a hedgehog defense. If you hadn't taken over, that position would have been overrun. We would've lost the hill and a lot more men. You saved more lives than we'll ever know."

"What I did seemed like the right thing to do. General Walker called me this morning. He read that report and wants me in his office when I'm released from the hospital to talk about it."

"Good." Mangus pointed at his chest. "I hope he's as impressed as me. You did an amazing job. Worthy of the name MacKenzie. Your dad and mom would be so proud of you. I just wish you'd joined the Marines."

"I'm nothing special. Just a grunt." Jackson changed the subject. "What happened to the major?"

"You mean the dumb ass. He started to apologize, but that's when you fell asleep. You know, he's one of their doctors. A pretty heartless one if you ask me."

"Me too. Heard he's a stickler for the regs. A real hard ass. That's good to a point but—"

"Not to a kid who just lost both parents. I filed a complaint with Army JAG about his unethical behavior. Bet he doesn't stay in the Army much longer. I also recommended he lose his medical license. He'll either be prosecuted or wind up the sanitation supervisor at Fort Wainwright in Alaska." Mangus checked his watch. "I need to go. Take it easy. I'll see you stateside after your tour." He squeezed Jackson's good shoulder. "Duck next time, please."

Jackson smiled. "Yes, sir."

Mangus stood. On his way out, the door opened. A middle-aged woman wearing fatigues with long salt and pepper hair in a ponytail came in.

"General," she said.

"Ma'am," Mangus replied.

She paused. "Are you Manny?"

Mangus cocked his head. "Yes, and you are?"

"Major Tina Mitchell. I'm the head nurse of the 8055th. Kim was my friend. We're all broken up about her death. She spoke of James, her sons, you, and Sara often. Talking about our families helped to get through the long days and even longer nights."

"I know that from experience, ma'am. James was my best friend. Jackson's my godson."

"Kim told me. Jim's godparents are her friends, Noah and Leslie Arnold." Tina approached the bed. "Need anything...squirt?"

Jackson felt the heat rise in his face. "So you know about that?"

"Yes, and the story behind it, but I'm not about to tell you."

Mangus laughed. "So do I. Behave yourself, Jackson. Remember, I can find out."

"Yes, sir," Jackson replied.

"I'll see you in a few months." Mangus left the room.

Tina sat in the chair. "Need anything?"

Jackson thought for a second. "Yeah, something besides hospital food."

"Like what?"

Only one thing came to mind. "A milkshake."

"I'll get you one and come back. I want to tell you how special Kim was to all of us."

"I already know, but I want to hear it anyway. I miss her." Jackson wiped away a tear. His mother was an angel. Always willing to lend a hand or help someone in distress. And give a hug when needed. Something he craved right now. Companionship. Someone to talk to and listen.

July 29, 1952
Chitose Air Base, Hokkaidō, Japan

Jackson climbed off the transport at the airfield. He jumped into the jeep waiting for him at the gate. It took him to the 1st Cavalry Division headquarters. He watched the scenery go by. A silver F-86 Sabre flashed by overhead and banked hard left, bringing his attention back to their location. Parked in front of headquarters.

A PFC met him on the sidewalk. "The general is waiting on you, Corporal MacKenzie."

"I'm not late, am I?" Jackson glanced at his watch. 1100. His meeting with General Walker was at 1130 hours.

"No. I'm your escort. Follow me."

The PFC led him to the same office where he had met with the general upon his arrival in Japan. He waited for his scheduled time in the outer office.

At precisely 1130 hours, the general's clerk, First Sergeant Katz, knocked on the inner door. A few seconds later, he opened it. "Go in, Corporal."

Jackson straightened his Ike jacket and went inside. He stopped in the center of the room. "Corporal MacKenzie reporting as ordered, sir."

General Walker nodded. "At ease, Corporal."

"Yes, sir." Jackson put his hands behind his back and spread his legs shoulder-width apart.

"Take a seat."

"Yes, sir." Jackson sat in the chair in front of him.

"First of all, I want to extend my condolences on the loss of your parents. I had no idea your father was Colonel James MacKenzie, the Medal of Honor recipient from the Battle of Okinawa. The commanding officer of the 1st Marines. Your mother was a brave woman for serving in a MASH unit. Her CO recommended her for the Silver Star and Purple

Heart. She distinguished herself at the aid station taking care of wounded under fire. The report says she saved the lives of a dozen men at the risk of her own."

"Really?" Jackson couldn't keep from blurting it out.

General Walker smiled. "Yes, really. You should be very proud of her."

"I am, sir." *More than you will ever know. Mom was a hero. Now she's an angel.*

"I'm sorry we couldn't get you home for the funeral. The doctors wouldn't allow it. I tried. You deserved to be there to accept their flags."

"Yes, sir. The doc wouldn't budge when I asked him. Said I needed to heal. General Malone tried too."

"I talked with him about you. He's your godfather, correct?"

"Yes, sir. I grew up with his kids. Why?"

"He's hell-bent on getting you into the Marine Corps." General Walker came around the desk and picked up a folder. "This is Captain Tiller's after-action report. It speaks highly of your actions on June 26th. You took over your platoon and led a successful defense of your position against two full Chinese companies. Excellent work."

"Yes, sir."

"What are your plans, Corporal?"

"Plans, sir?"

"After the war. You enlisted for two years."

Ah-ha! "I want to go to West Point, sir," Jackson announced proudly.

"West Point, excellent choice. Why did you enlist? You have an automatic appointment."

Jackson nodded. "Yes, sir, I do. I want to make it on my own merit. That's why I enlisted. Dad casts…cast a pretty big shadow in the Corps. So does General Malone. I don't want to get there by riding their coattails. I want to do it completely on my own. No preferential treatment."

"Like I said the day we met, there's officer material in you. What were your grades in high school?" General Walker asked.

"Straight As. I worked hard to graduate a year early."

"That goes with your induction test scores. Off the charts. The top of every percentile. Have you ever taken an IQ test?"

"No, sir."

"Well, I don't need to know what your IQ is, but I know it's high."

"Yes, sir, if you say so."

"Would you be agreeable to me sending a personal recommendation to the Chief of Staff and the President for your acceptance into West Point next fall?"

Jackson almost jumped out of his chair. "Yes, sir. Thank you, sir."

"No. Thank you, Corporal. I mean that. It's rare to find someone so young with such natural leadership ability and intelligence. You'll go far. Maybe even as far as being Chief of Staff yourself someday."

Since he couldn't tell his superior officer *no*, Jackson nodded. "If you say so, sir."

"I do. I'll send a request to Camp Pendleton to have your school records forwarded to West Point. All of this is dependent on those. Did you play any sports?"

"Yes, sir. I rode equestrian for years. Eventing, jumping, and dressage. I played baseball in high school and ran track. Set the school records. I did 1:55 in the 880-yard run, 4:20 in the mile and I was team captain."

"Excellent. What sport do you want to try out for?"

That was an easy question. "Equestrian. I'm a pretty good middle-distance runner, but I'm even better on the back of a horse. At home, I have a room full of blue ribbons and trophies."

"I'll add that to your packet and request those records too…and I'll be adding this. Stand up, Corporal."

Jackson stood in front of his chair and looked over his shoulder.

The general opened the inner office door. Several men in Army uniforms came in. General Gatlin, the CO of the 25th Infantry Division, Colonel Skinner, CO of the 27th Infantry Regiment, Lieutenant Colonel Barton, CO of the 2nd Battalion, and Captain Zeller, his company commander.

"Attention to orders," General Walker commanded.

Jackson snapped to attention.

General Walker pulled a piece of paper from a folder on his desk. "The Army Distinguished Service Cross is hereby awarded to Corporal Jackson J. MacKenzie, US Army, 1st Cavalry Division, TDY to Easy Company, 2nd Battalion, 27th Infantry Regiment, 25th Infantry Division. For extraordinary heroism in action at Old Baldy, Hill 266 on 26 June 1952. While 1st Platoon was occupying an exposed front line position under heavy mortar attack and machine-gun fire, Corporal MacKenzie assumed command after Lieutenant Wheeler and the senior enlisted men were killed. Under his command, the platoon repelled several waves of strong enemy attacks on their position. Even after being wounded in the chest, Corporal MacKenzie maintained his position on the line. He led by example, saving the lives of the remaining members of the platoon and countless others by repelling the advance. This assisted the other units engaged with the enemy to maintain possession of Hill 266. Corporal

MacKenzie's heroism and selflessness above and beyond the call of duty are in keeping with the highest traditions of military service and reflect great credit upon himself and the United States Army."

Wow, didn't expect that. Jackson puffed out his chest, straightened his back, and tucked in his chin.

General Walker opened a blue presentation case, pulled out a blue and red ribbon holding a bronze cross with an eagle in the center, and pinned it to Jackson's Ike jacket. He turned back to the desk. When he faced him again, the general had a Purple Heart in his hand. "This is for being wounded in action." He pinned it next to the DSC. "At ease."

Jackson placed his hands behind his back and spread his feet shoulder-width apart. "Thank you, sir."

"It's my honor, young man. I hate to do this to you. Again. I want you under my command but so does General Gatlin and right now after what happened, they are short. Give it a few weeks and I promise to get rid of the TDY status. These medals will put you over the top. Between us, plan on being at West Point next summer."

"Yes, sir."

General Gatlin gripped Jackson's shoulder. "It's an honor to have you under my command, MacKenzie. Even if it's just for a few weeks." He pulled a set of sergeant's stripes from his pocket. "Congratulations, Sergeant MacKenzie."

"Yes, sir." *This day keeps getting better.* Jackson couldn't stand any taller. He was on top of the world.

"Go with them, son. Their driver has your bag. You will be hearing from me soon."

"Yes, sir." Jackson followed the officers out of the room. He was headed back into the combat zone. The peace and quiet was nice while it lasted. Now he had more work to do.

CHAPTER 5

August 1, 1952 – 0200 hours
Main camp of the 25th Infantry Division

"Mooo…"

The plop of hooves on the soft ground reached Jackson's ears. He looked into the valley. A herd of cows were near his guard position at the edge of camp. Curious, he slung his M1, grabbed the binoculars from the guard shack, and focused on the herd. Hanwoo cattle. A species native to Korea. Unlike the Hereford cattle he knew so well, brown with white faces, these cattle were mixed colors, brown, brindle, and black.

The cattle moved slowly across the field, chewing cud and grazing on the green grass. Since there was nothing unusual about cattle in the area, he put down his binoculars.

Several of the cows spooked and moved away from one in the middle of the herd. Almost as if running from a predator. Backs arched, heads and ears lowered and tensed in a defensive posture.

Jackson put the binoculars back to his eyes and focused on the one cow. It not only looked funny, loose floppy skin on a very skinny cow, but it moved funny. Not the smooth motion of something used to four legs and hooves. Everything was uncoordinated, jerky, and slow. The rear legs didn't look right. The knees were in the wrong spot. Pointing forward, not backward.

Another cow bumped into the strange one. Spinning it around. The front half went down then the back half. A few seconds later, the front half stood then the back half. Not anything like how a cow would stand up. Only one thing came to mind—a cow suit with humans inside.

Jackson got on the field telephone and called for backup. He unslung his M1, put the stock to his shoulder, and went down to where the cows crossed the road. And waited.

As the herd lumbered past him, he watched the strange cow. The head was too square and the eyes fixed black glass orbs. Lifeless. When it got to the edge of the dirt road, he raised his M1, stepped out of the shadow of a large tree, and put the muzzle between the cow's eyes. "Hands up!" he said in English. To make sure they understood, he said it in Korean too. "Son deul-eo."

The brown leather cow suit split apart in the middle. Two Asian men wearing North Korean lieutenant's uniforms put their hands up.

40

Two soldiers ran up to him. "What is it, Sergeant?" one of them said.

"Take my spot. Both of you. Stay frosty. They might not be the only ones."

The men jogged to the guard shack.

Jackson waved at the road with his M1. "March... haengjin."

The two North Koreans, cow suit and all, walked into the road.

Jackson stayed behind them, poking the rear man in the back with his M1 muzzle. "Keep going... gyesogga." *Thank you, Lieutenant Quinton, for the handbook on simple phrases.* He marched them all the way to headquarters.

Two MPs met him at the doors. "What's going on, Sergeant MacKenzie?"

"Infiltrators. Call Captain Zeller. Get him and anyone else who wants to join the party down here." Jackson motioned at the steps with his rifle. "Sit... anjda."

The two men sat down and started removing the cow suit.

Jackson stuck his rifle muzzle in the middle of the closest one's eyes and shook his head. "No." He wanted everyone to see them wearing a cow suit.

A few minutes later, Captain Zeller and Major Overton ran up.

"Well, well. Look what MacKenzie caught," Captain Zeller said. "Good job, Sergeant." He waved at the MPs. "We'll take it from here."

Jackson slung his M1. "Yes, sir. I'm still on watch, so I'll head back."

"Who replaced you?"

"Washington and the new guy, Private Kunzweiler."

"They can finish your watch. Go grab some rack time. You earned it."

Never one to tell a superior officer *no* or pass up extra sleep, Jackson came to attention. "Yes, sir." He headed to the barracks, ready to make love to his pillow.

August 5, 1952

Jackson led his squad on patrol along a creek bed near the 38th parallel, next to the Jamestown defensive line. The night was pitch-black and angry, not a star seen in the sky through the low-hanging clouds. The air heavy with moisture, soaking everything though no rain was present.

Lieutenant Quinton had him looking for possible new enemy emplacements, rumored by intelligence to be popping up in the area. No one was beyond suspicion, not even civilians in makeshift encampments. The North Korean Army was known for dressing like them to take

Americans by surprise. Fake pregnant women wearing bombs under their garments. Old men with hidden rifles and machine guns. And one that turned his stomach, booby-trapping the bodies of dead American soldiers.

"Halt," the point man, Private Giovanni, called out.

Jackson held up his hand, bringing his men to a halt. He belly crawled up to Gino, an M1 rifle in the crook of his elbows, the grenades on his flak jacket scraping the dirt. "What have you got?" he whispered.

"Not sure." Gino pointed at a glow in the distance. "Look like a campfire to you?"

Jackson pushed back his helmet. "Hmm." He sniffed. A faint hint of wood smoke was in the air. "Yeah. Go up quietly. See if it's a friendly or a gook, patrol."

"Yes, sir." Gino crawled ahead, disappearing into the brush.

Jackson waved his men forward until they were lined up behind him. "Hooper, watch our six," he whispered.

"Sure, Sarge."

They waited for Gino to return. It seemed to take forever until his dirty form finally emerged from the brush.

"Gooks, Sarge. Not a patrol. Looks like a damn stinking platoon. At least fifty men. Might be more. Maybe a company...or bigger. Can't see much beyond the light of their outer guards' fire."

"Hmm...radio," Jackson whispered. Removing the map from his pocket, he held up a flashlight and checked their coordinates. With the ammo they had, a squad didn't have a chance against fifty men—let alone possibly two hundred.

Private Spangler, his radioman, crawled up. "Here, Sarge."

Jackson yanked the handset off the radio pack and keyed up. "Ghost one-two to Ghost one-six."

"Go ahead, Ghost one-two, this is actual," said a crackly voice.

"Found possible enemy platoon or company. Requesting artillery strike. Grid coordinates, three-zero...three-one."

"Sorry, Ghost one-two, all batteries are currently engaged. The best I can do is an airstrike. Can it be spotted from the air?"

"Affirmative. They have at least one fire going, maybe more. Couldn't get close enough to determine size."

"Roger. Will call it in. Sit tight. Be the ground spotter for the incoming aircraft."

"Message acknowledged. Out." Jackson handed the handset back to Spangler. "Now we wait. Spread the word behind you. Eat your rations. No talking."

Minutes ticked by. They turned into an hour, then almost two. Crickets chirped, mosquitos buzzed, frogs croaked. The darkness slowly faded away as the time crept toward dawn.

The faint roar of piston engines broke through the natural sounds. Jackson looked into the sky east of his position. He could barely make out the planes as the morning light glinted off the silver wings. Two P-51 Mustangs. Both laden down with bombs and rockets. He grabbed the radio handset. "Ghost one-two to Overwatch."

"Overwatch one here. Mark your position with red smoke. Don't want to hit you. I see the fires. Say goodbye to the gooks."

"Acknowledged." Jackson turned to Spangler. "Pop a red smoke."

"Roger." Spangler threw a smoke canister in front of them. Red smoke blanketed the area. Blowing across them in the wind.

"Got your smoke. Put your heads down. This might get close and hot."

"Out." Jackson put down the handset. "Get down and cover!" he yelled over his shoulder.

The Mustangs flew over low and fast. So low, Jackson felt the prop wash. He placed his hands over his ears to protect them.

In front of them, two hundred yards away, the green of the forest turned yellow then red. The blast wave hit him a second later, along with the ear-popping bang of the explosion. It rattled the fillings in his teeth. The fireball rolled closer but stopped fifty yards from their position. It had gotten close—and hot.

"Ghost one-two, this is Overwatch. You still here?"

"Roger, Overwatch. Any movement?" Jackson replied.

"Hold on, let me do a flyover."

Jackson watched the two Mustangs swoop low over the area then climb back to around two thousand feet.

"Ghost one-two. No movement. Good for you to move in."

"Roger. Out." Jackson gave the handset back to Spangler. He stood and waved his men forward. "Move out."

Even with the assurance from the pilot, Jackson and his men entered the encampment with rifles at the ready. Nothing moved. No animals, birds, or insects. Smoke drifted on the breeze, and the stench of death filled the air.

All around them, in the blackened and still-smoking forest, men lay, some burned beyond recognition, some moaning, still alive but not for long. Some had no marks at all, killed by the blast wave, and some shredded by the shrapnel.

43

Jackson knelt beside one man who was barely alive. The soldier, a Chinese captain from the rank on his collar, opened his eyes. They were brown and blood-shot, the pupils wide and black.

He grabbed Jackson's arm but Jackson jerked it away, not wanting the enemy to touch him. It felt creepy. Wet. Gooey. Slimy. The skin of the man's palm slid off and fell to the ground. Cooked flesh flaking off the finger bones.

The man looked at him, his eyes pleading. He moaned the rasping rattle of someone taking one of their last breaths. Jackson clamped down on his revulsion, grabbed his hand, and held it tight. The captain's grip tightened then lessened and went limp, but his eyes remained open, glazed over and staring straight ahead.

Jackson closed them then checked the man's uniform for papers or anything of value. This was an officer, and they needed intelligence.

Spangler approached him. "Sarge?"

"Yeah." Jackson looked at his radioman. "Sit-rep."

"Anyone still alive won't be for long. Looks like an entire company was encamped. Orders?"

"Have everyone start digging. Bury the dead. Check all clothing for identification, maps, and other papers. Give those to me. I'll take them to headquarters when we get back to camp." Jackson tucked the ID papers and maps from the dead captain into his shirt. He pulled out his entrenching tool. They had a long day ahead of them before heading back to camp. The first thing he would do, take a shower and wash the unforgettable smell of death from him—his person, his clothing. He didn't think he would ever get it out of his nose.

August 6, 1952 – 0230 hours

Boom! Boom! Boom! Everything vibrated. Rat-a-tat… Machine-gun fire blasted everything around him. The soppy, humid air felt electrically charged. He could smell smoke, nitroglycerin, gunpowder, and gasoline. *Sneak attack.* Jackson rolled off his bunk onto the floor, scrambling for his M1 rifle propped against the wall.

The squad bay was dark but not pitch-black, lit by a single emergency light over the door. Black-out curtains kept any outside light from coming into the barracks.

Burned faces floated in front of him. Glazed-over eyes stared at him. The metallic odor of blood and cooked flesh filled his nose. He could feel the heat still radiating from the bodies on the ground in front of him. Jackson shook his head. "No...no...no..."

The images of burned bodies faded into the darkened squad bay. The stench of death became the typical smell of the barracks. Dirty laundry, gun oil, bleach, and...body odor. *Just a bad dream.*

Jackson looked over the blanket-covered mounds of his men, all still asleep and snoring. He lowered his rifle, took a breath, and stood. After propping his rifle against the wall, he dressed in his fatigues hung over his bunk frame and slipped on his combat boots. He picked up his rifle, slung an ammo bandoleer over his shoulder, put on his helmet, and left the barracks. His soul needed some air.

With nowhere to go, he walked across the compound. *Might as well check the watch.* At each station stood a guard, ever vigilant, making sure no one unauthorized entered the camp. Protecting them in their sleep. Since the mess tent always had coffee for the men on duty, Jackson headed there.

A light inside one tent made him pause. In front of the entrance sat a two-foot wooden cross on a pedestal. With the flap open, Jackson approached and knocked on the tent support.

"Come in," said a deep male voice with an Irish accent.

Jackson went inside. He nodded at the Army chaplain, Captain Donnelly, seated at a small table.

Donnelly put down his pencil. "Sergeant MacKenzie. To what do I owe the pleasure of your company in the wee hours of the morning?"

"Ahh..." Jackson glanced at his watch. 0330. "Sorry for bothering you. I can come back at a more convenient time."

"No, please sit. You look troubled, son. And you're not intruding. I'm just working on my sermon for Sunday. Glad for a break." Donnelly scooted his chair around to face him.

Jackson sat in front of the chaplain. "Well..." He stopped then slid out of the chair onto his knees and hung his head. "Forgive me, Father, for I have sinned."

Donnelly placed a hand on Jackson's shoulder. "Sit in the chair, MacKenzie. Talk to me."

"I gotta do this first."

"No, talk to me. I want to look you in the eyes, not at the top of your head."

"Okay." Jackson returned to his chair.

"Now, tell me what happened since mass last Sunday."

Jackson cleared his throat. "A lot…I called in an airstrike on a Chinese company."

"And?"

"They all died. I can't sleep. They keep staring at me. I keep smelling death. Seeing their blackened faces. Feeling the explosions. Listening to them moaning. That damn death rattle won't go away. Sorry."

"Don't worry. Not the first time I've heard that. Why do you think you've sinned?"

"My orders killed those men. Burned them alive. They died a horrible death. Cooking like barbecued pigs. I wouldn't wish that on anyone. Not even gooks."

"Did you save lives by doing it?" Donnelly asked.

"Probably. None of my men died. No one was wounded." Jackson knew his actions had saved lives, but his decision burned men alive. They died a painful, agonizing death.

"Is that it, or is something else bothering you?"

"Yeah. I know as soldiers we have to kill. I took an oath that says I will defend the United States Constitution against all enemies, foreign and domestic, but…"

"As a Catholic, you're having a hard time reconciling it. Is that your sin? You've had to kill, so you feel like a murderer. It's not any of the others, right?" Donnelly pointed at his purple stole hanging on the coat rack. "No stealing? No adultery? No taking the lord's name in vain?"

"No."

"Okay, young man. I applaud your conscience. It's nice to see our beautiful country can produce soldiers who are patriotic but who can also question what they've been taught. Now, let me explain. The Fifth Commandment, translated, means, 'I shall not murder.' There's a difference between killing and murder."

Jackson was confused. "They're the same thing. You're just as dead. Food for the maggots in a shallow hole."

"No." Donnelly rubbed the cross around his neck. "Killing is the taking of any life, even that of animals for food. If the lord meant that all death is wrong, there wouldn't be armies to defend the weak and we would starve without the meat of living things to sustain us."

Jackson cocked his head. It was an enlightening idea, one he hadn't thought about. "Still…"

"Sergeant, as a soldier, you have to kill, but it's not murder. Think of it as…self-defense. It's no different morally than defending your loved ones from an attack by an assailant at home. Would you call your father a murderer for defending your mother against a rapist if he beat the man to death or shot him?"

"No, sir." Jackson sniffed. The chaplain was new, having arrived two weeks ago and had no idea his parents were dead. Maybe that was part of his problem. His heart and soul were still reeling from their deaths.

"A just war is defined by two theological ideas. First, the reasons for going to war must be just and honorable."

"And the second?"

"The way the war is fought must be just and honorable. Done for reasons to save others and to make sure they don't become a statistic. A blip in the radar of history. If you followed the rules of engagement set forth by your commanding officers and used the methods made available to you, like the planes and bombs, in the manner they are meant. Not in anger or revenge. If you made sure to avoid harming the non-combatants and prisoners of war, then—"

"There were no prisoners of war. I killed them all. Death by fire and shrapnel."

"Let me finish. Any killing done is justified to secure the victory of the righteous. War is horrible and tragic, but sometimes it's necessary for the greater good. So, in what I have said, are you a murderer?"

"No, sir."

"Do you still need absolution from your sins?"

To live with himself, Jackson had only one answer. "Yes." He'd killed. There was no way around it.

"Okay. To make you feel better. Kneel." Donnelly placed the purple stole around his neck as Jackson got down on his knees and bowed his head. "I absolve you from your sins, in the name of the Father, and of the Son, and the Holy Spirit."

"Amen." Jackson crossed himself and returned to his chair.

Donnelly sat in his, leaned forward, and gripped Jackson's shoulder. "Now, tell me what's really bothering you?"

Jackson took a deep breath. He had to do this. "My dad and mom died."

"When?"

"June 26th."

"Where?"

"Here in Korea."

"MacKenzie...MacKenzie..." Donnelly snapped his fingers. "As in Major MacKenzie, a nurse at the MASH unit, and her husband? They're your parents?"

"Yes, sir." Jackson brushed a hand across his eyes.

47

Donnelly smiled. "Okay, son. Let's talk. But I can already tell what you're feeling is survivor's guilt. You're here, but they aren't. Just tell me everything. Including what happened to you that day."

Jackson looked around. He had a hard time admitting this to anyone, especially himself. Growing up sure was hard. More challenging than he'd ever thought it would be. It would be so much easier to be a kid again and forget the horrors of the real world. "We were called to reinforce Old Baldy. I was nervous…no, scared. I was afraid I would freeze. I forced my fear down, took over the platoon, and did my job…"

August 19, 1952 – 0000 hours
Bridge over the Bukhan River
Jamestown Line, North of the 38th Parallel

Red flares lit the night sky and explosions like rolling thunder rocked the bridge. The supports shook in their foundations, bending and creaking from strain. Jackson wondered about the stability of the bridge. It might collapse from under them.

With what was left of his ten-man squad, Jackson knelt behind the overturned donkey cart reinforced with sandbags. He pointed his M1 rifle at the Chinese troops grouped on the other side of the bridge. The Thompson sub-machine gun he pulled from Corporal Hawkins' body was propped on the cart next to his feet. His orders, hold the bridge at all costs.

Two of his men lay dead behind him, their bodies covered with poncho liners. Farther back with the medic, two others lay on the bridge deck, moaning in pain. The six men he had left were lined up behind the donkey cart and the sandbags to the right of it.

He stuck his bayonet on the muzzle of his M1. Today might be the day he got to use the techniques he'd learned in basic training on dummies stuffed with straw. Except these men were alive. They could fight back with bayonets of their own.

To his right, Corporal Pagano manned their one .50-caliber Browning machine gun. Private Hooker had the BAR ready to rock and roll. Private Horowitz had wired the bridge supports with explosives in case their position was overrun. There was no way Jackson would allow that to happen. He had his orders, and they would hold this bridge.

They had one advantage. The bridge's narrow superstructure forced anyone who crossed it shoulder to shoulder into a fatal funnel, right into their kill zone. The BAR on the right and .50 caliber Browning on the left with interlocking fields of fire. The surviving members of the squad made up the middle with their small arms. M1s, pistols, three cases of grenades, and one Thompson sub-machine gun.

Jackson yanked the handset off the pack of his radioman, PFC Spangler. "Ghost one-two to Ghost one-six."

After a few seconds of static came the reply. "Go Ghost one-two, this is actual."

"Taking fire. Mortar and machine guns. Two dead. Two wounded. Need the rest of the platoon up here. At least a company in front of us, maybe more."

"Sorry, Ghost one-two. No can do. Engaged just north of your position. I'll relay the message to the captain. I'll see if we can get the 8th or 64th Artillery to send up a spotter and give you some support. The 90th and 159th are engaged with us. Out."

Jackson gave the handset back to Spangler. "Well, we're on our own." He knew the Chinese weren't about to mortar the bridge. They wanted it whole. Blowing it up wouldn't do them any good.

"Yes, sir." Spangler leveled his M1 over the donkey cart.

Minutes ticked by. The Chinese kept massing on the other side of the bridge, just out of visual range in the darkness. But Jackson could hear the murmur of voices, the rustle of clothing and footsteps.

Then came the bugle blasts, signaling advance.

A squad of Chinese soldiers appeared through the fog. They marched slowly over the bridgehead, their bolt-action rifles with bayonets attached in a ready stance for hand-to-hand combat.

"Make every shot count," Jackson called to his men.

The Chinese soldiers got closer and closer. Just the one squad. Ten men.

They're testing our defensive setup. "Pagano, Hooker, hold fire. Save your ammo for when they charge us. Guys, one shot, one kill," Jackson said to his men. He aimed right at the heart of the soldier directly in front of him. At twenty-five yards away, he put a round directly into the man's chest. That close, the .30-06 armor-piercing round blew a hole the size of a baseball out of his back. Blood spurted into the air in a cloudy mist and the man dropped.

His squad opened fire. Each shot found its mark. The entire Chinese squad dropped in their tracks, falling into a pile, one on top of the other.

What's next? Jackson waited anxiously. There were no reinforcements, and an eerie uneasy silence enveloped the night. Not even a cricket chirped. The gunfire had scared everything away.

Machine-gun fire started from the Chinese side. Everyone ducked behind cover.

White-hot pain exploded in his calf and up into his brain. Jackson realized his right leg was stuck across the open crack between the sandbags and the donkey cart. He jerked his leg behind cover. "Shit!" *I'm an idiot.*

The medic ran up. "Are you hit, Sergeant?"

"Yeah…Pagano, keep an eye on them. Sing out if someone else comes." Jackson sat down. There was a hole on both sides of his trouser leg. A trickle of blood coated the bridge deck and his trousers.

The medic examined his leg. "It's a through and through."

"Bandage it over my uniform. I have to stay on the line."

"You sure?" the medic asked.

"Yes, I'm sure. Unless you're going to take over, Kershaw?"

Kershaw laughed. "Not in my job description." He dusted sulfanilamide on the wounds then wrapped a four-inch gauze bandage around the outside of Jackson's trousers. "Can you stand?"

"Let's see. Help me up." Jackson grabbed Kershaw's extended hand and stood. He tested his right leg by putting weight on it. *Oww…oww…oww.* Pain went up his spine but his leg held. At least for now. "Go tend to the wounded, Kershaw. I've got this." He returned to his position, picked up his M1, and aimed downrange.

The gunfire stopped abruptly again, and things fell into an uncomfortable silence.

Another squad appeared. They did the same thing. Marched toward them with rifles and bayonets extended.

Jackson and his men waited until they reached the dead Chinese soldiers before firing. These men dropped onto the pile with the others. *At least they're building a wall to climb over.*

The silence came again. It lasted for thirty minutes. A bright searchlight came on, lighting up their position. Then came a voice over a loudspeaker.

"Surrender. You are only delaying the inevitable. We know you have no reinforcements. They are occupied on the other side of the valley."

The Chinese were trying to psych them out. Good old head manipulation. It wouldn't work on him or his men. They had been in battle together and survived. His men were tough. The simple tricks of psychological warfare wouldn't work on them.

"Come on over. We don't bite," Jackson yelled over the donkey cart. He aimed for the center of the glare and fired. The light went out to the sound of shattered glass, sparks, and screams of pain.

Again, more silence. But it didn't last. Men massed at the bridgehead. Instead of standing like statues, these men bounced up and down on their feet. They were ready to fight. Ready to charge.

Jackson glanced to his right and left. Pagano charged his Browning, and Hooker did the same with the BAR. The rest of the squad leaned into the shoulder stocks of their rifles. They were ready.

A bugle blasted and the massed troops ran at them. Once inside the kill zone, the BAR and Browning .50 opened up. A dozen men went down immediately and the next wave climbed over them. Shots from the M1s took down six more.

In need of more firepower, Jackson reached next to his leg for the Thompson.

Screams of incoming shells pierced the air, landing on the massed troops at the bridgehead. Fireballs rose into the night. The 25th DIVARTY had just saved the day.

Jackson pointed the Thompson at the enemy and opened fire on full auto, screaming his war cry—as the drill instructors had called it at the top of his lungs. "Aaahhh…" His rapid shots cut any man close to him in a Chinese uniform into ribbons. He didn't care how many men he killed. They all needed to die. That was the way of war. All gooks to him. Those men wanted to kill him. He felt the same way, except he and his men would be standing at the end. Alive.

Caught between them and the artillery, the troops stopped in their tracks. Either direction meant death. The Chinese side turned into a massive fireball as explosions rocked the ground and the bridge.

Jackson and his men kept firing. Steam rose from the hot rifle barrels into the humid night air.

As suddenly as it started the shelling stopped. Smoke lay in a thick blanket across the bridge. The fires slowly died out, dropping the ambient lighting to almost nothing. Minutes passed, and the breeze started blowing the smoke away. The moon appeared, then the bodies became visible. A veritable carpet of men in tattered, blood-covered Chinese uniforms. They couldn't walk without stepping on one. The breeze blew the smoke out and the nasty stench of charred bodies in. An almost nauseating smell. Death. Carnage. Destruction. Iron. Cooked flesh. Anyone still alive wouldn't be for long.

Jackson grabbed the handset Spangler handed him. "Ghost one-two to Ghost one-six."

"Go ahead, Ghost one-two. This is actual."

"Who was that, the 8th or the 64th?"

"Both."

"Tell them they did some mighty fine shooting," Jackson said, looking at the piles of bodies.

"Will do. Do you need assistance?"

"Not now with the bridge. We can hold it until 1st squad gets here. Send the helicopters. I have wounded who need to be evac'd."

"Roger. Reinforcements are on their way. Good job, Ghost one-two. Relay that to your men."

"Yes, sir. Out." Jackson gave the handset back to Spangler. He cautiously stepped around the donkey cart, the M1 slung across his back, and the Thompson pointed into the darkness. His leg ached, but it was nothing he couldn't handle.

Slowly, he limped to the closest soldier. The man was young, very young. He couldn't have been over seventeen at the most. Jackson did a double-take. The kid was the same age as him and had to have hopes and dreams too. Not of war, of life. A family, kids, and maybe even a dog. It made him feel creepy inside. A cold shiver ran down his spine.

No, he wanted to kill me. He got what he deserved. Jackson shook his head. He had to look at it that way. Death was a part of war. Part of a soldier's life. This was his dream, and no one would take it from him. Still, part of his heart wept for the kid who never would follow his path in life. Live out his hopes and dreams. Be happy.

August 21, 1952
121st Medical Evacuation Hospital – Seoul, South Korea

Jackson looked up from his book, *Boot: A Marine in the Making* by Gilbert P. Bailey, when his door opened. It had surprised him an Army hospital had a library book about Marines, but reading would help him pass the time.

General Walker came in.

Jackson sat up straighter in his bed and put the book down. "Sir."

General Walker smiled. "Relax. You don't have to sit at attention. I was in Seoul and wanted to check on you."

"Yes, sir." He was still uncomfortable. The last time a general visited him…Uncle Manny…it was for bad news.

"You did an excellent job on that bridge. And got yourself shot again."

"Yes, sir. This isn't as bad as it looks." Jackson massaged his right leg propped up on a pillow. It itched more than hurt under the mound of bandages. The damn morphine made sure he didn't feel much. *At least I don't have an IV or Foley anymore.*

"Typical for an Airborne guy. I talked to your doctor. It might be a through and through, but that round did a lot of damage. You're going to be in the hospital on crutches for two weeks and on injury leave for two more."

"Yes, sir. The doc told me already."

"I contacted General Malone."

Shit! "What did he say?"

"You didn't duck far enough. I told him you'll be fine. He's not going to tell Sara."

"Whew." Jackson breathed a sigh of relief. "Good."

General Walker sat in the chair next to the bed. "He didn't want her to worry."

"Yeah, she would too."

"MacKenzie, consider your TDY status over. I want you under my command. Once you're released back to duty, I'm placing you in the 8th Cavalry Regiment. You'll be under Lieutenant Simmons in 1st Platoon, Fox Company, 2nd Battalion."

"Yes, sir. Thank you, sir."

"I'll have your orders cut. They'll be delivered once you're cleared for duty. Until then, MacKenzie, relax and enjoy the downtime. Once you get under me, I'll work your butt off. I want you ready for West Point. I'm confident you'll be on the list when it comes out. They always hold a few slots in reserve for enlisted personnel recommended for admittance by their commanding officers. I'm not the only one who submitted a letter to the board."

"Really? Who else did?"

"General Malone, General Gatlin, Colonel Skinner, and…General MacArthur."

"General MacArthur? Really?"

"Yes. He heard about your actions at Old Baldy through the Army grapevine and requested the report. After reading it, he called me. I told him about your plans, your intelligence, and your father. He was impressed that you didn't use the automatic appointment and felt duty-bound to help you. You have people in your corner. Now you just have to stay alive. No more of this." The general pointed at the bed.

"No, sir. I intend to avoid hospital stays at all costs." Jackson nodded at the door. "The nurses won't leave me alone. They watch everything."

He hated peeing into a bedpan in front of a girl. It was embarrassing for them to see his penis, balls, and bare butt hanging out of a hospital gown.

General Walker laughed. "I know. Been in your position for an appendectomy. When you get to Japan, report to my office. We'll talk more then. Take it easy, Sergeant. I left word with the docs to call if you don't follow their orders. Am I clear?"

"Crystal, sir. No problems."

"Good. Didn't expect any." General Walker picked up the book. "Like military history?"

"Yes, sir, and stuff about horses."

"I have a few military books in my quarters. I'll send them over in the mail run. Don't have any about horses."

"Thank you, sir. The chaplain said he'd look around for some."

"Expect to be worked hard the next time I see you."

"Yes, sir," Jackson said with enthusiasm. MacArthur had sent a letter to the acceptance board. General Douglas MacArthur. The man awarded the Medal of Honor for the defense of the Philippines. The man who accepted the surrender of Japan on the U.S.S. Missouri. Supreme Commander for the Allied Powers for the occupation of Japan. The first Commander-in-Chief of the United Nations Command for the Korean War. Maybe he did have a real chance to go to West Point next summer. To follow in his father's footsteps and serve his country with honor as an officer.

CHAPTER 6

September 18, 1952
Chitose Air Base, Hokkaidō, Japan

Jackson wiped his sweaty palms on his OD wool uniform pants as he waited outside General Walker's office. Even though the general had told him that his TDY status was now null and void, anything could change. The war wasn't ending anytime soon. He really wanted to spend part of his tour with the 1st Cavalry Division. The First Team.

At precisely 1300 hours, the general's clerk, First Sergeant Katz, opened the inner door. "He's ready for you, Sergeant."

Jackson nodded, marched into the office, and came to attention. "Sergeant MacKenzie reporting as ordered, sir."

"At ease, MacKenzie, sit down."

"Yes, sir." Jackson sat in the chair in front of the desk.

General Walker came around and sat on the edge of the desk. He picked up a piece of paper and handed it to him. "Here are your orders, 1st Platoon, Fox Company, 2nd Battalion. You'll be taking over as 3rd Squad sergeant. My aide has already taken your gear from Korea to the barracks. Enjoy the evening at the NCO club. It'll be your last night of relaxation until you get to know your men. The division may be in reserve but we're also here to defend Hokkaidō and to maintain maximum combat readiness. You haven't done an amphibious landing yet. Lieutenant Simmons will get you squared away in the techniques. Knowing how fast you learn, it'll only take once."

"Yes, sir." Jackson smiled inwardly. He was gaining experience and high-ranking friends by leaps and bounds. This training would only extend his Army resume.

"I got a call from the admittance board. Your recommendation and application are being fast-tracked for selection in next year's class. Now, this is unofficial, the board is impressed by your grades, athletic achievements, and performance in combat. The equestrian team needs two new riders and your list of wins at some huge meets is impressive. The coach has already put in a word that if you make selection, he wants you to try out. That's rare for a plebe."

"Yes, sir." *Maybe I'll get to ride again. Hope the horse is as good as Taco.*

"Any questions so far? Relax. Let's just talk so I can get to know you."

Even not wanting to get his hopes up, Jackson decided to ask anyway. "What do you think of my chances, sir?"

"Good. Come July 1953, R-day, you'll be meeting a cadet in the red sash."

"Huh?" Jackson cocked his head in confusion.

"R-day is reception day. As for the other, you'll find out. It's my strong belief you'll be part of the class of 1957. In fact, I'd call it a certainty but—"

"Don't get my hopes up because anything can happen."

"Yes, and usually does. I just don't see you being denied. Not with your service record and the people in your corner. You're more qualified than most of the current cadets and you could already be there anyway. It would be stupid not to select you."

"I appreciate your support and confidence in me, sir."

"If I wasn't so sure and had a slot available, I'd have given you a battlefield promotion to Second Lieutenant months ago. The only problem is your age. It might stick in the craw of my superiors."

"Yeah, not too many seventeen-year-old lieutenants."

"Exactly. How many languages do you speak?"

"Including English, three. I learned German and Spanish in high school."

"German is good. Interested in any others?"

"Yes, Russian. With the communists trying to take over the world, I thought that might be a good one to learn. You're asking for a reason, right?"

"Good observation. Yes. One person on the board wanted me to ask."

"Did this person want to know anything else?"

"Yes. He wanted a detailed rundown on what happened at Old Baldy." Jackson cocked his head. "Really?"

"Yes. I think you're going to drive your tactics instructors crazy. You're smarter than they are and could probably teach the class with them as the students."

"I learned a lot from Dad's stories about WWII."

General Walker laughed. "I think it's more than that. I'll get a date set up for you to take the West Point Achievement tests in Mathematics and English and the aptitude test. You'll need to take those for approval. Think you can pass them?"

"Yes, sir." *Hope so. Been out of school for almost a year now.*

"Good. Now I have a duty to perform before you leave."

Jackson looked behind him. The door was open. In the opening were General Gatlin, Colonel Skinner, Lt. Colonel Barton, and Captain Zeller. They came in and stood directly behind him.

"Attention to orders," General Walker commanded.

Jackson stood and came to attention.

"These men wanted to witness this. We feel that in a few years, you'll be our best and brightest star on the horizon." General Walker picked up a piece of paper from his desk. "The Silver Star is hereby awarded to Sergeant Jackson J. MacKenzie, US Army, 1st Cavalry Division. For conspicuous gallantry and intrepidity while serving TDY in 2nd Squad, 1st Platoon, Easy Company, 2nd Battalion, 27th Infantry Regiment, 25th Infantry Division. On 15 August 1952, while defending a bridge over the Bukhan river maintaining the Jamestown line, Sergeant MacKenzie's squad came under direct enemy fire by a superior hostile force. Sergeant MacKenzie distinguished himself by his heroic actions when two full Chinese companies tried to take control of the bridge through heavy machine-gun fire, mortar, and human wave attacks. With superior tactics and leadership, Sergeant MacKenzie directed his squad into a defensible position even after taking casualties. The seven men, including Sergeant MacKenzie, maintained control of the bridge through superior tactics instead of firepower until supported by an artillery barrage by batteries of the 8th and 64th artillery battalions. Even though wounded during the engagement, Sergeant MacKenzie maintained his position of leadership. Approximately ninety-five Chinese soldiers died trying to take the bridge. Forty-five of those are attributed to the men of 2nd Squad. Sergeant MacKenzie's brave actions and expert leadership helped to maintain our defensive line, thereby reducing casualties and saving lives. His fearless initiative, determined fortitude, and unwavering devotion to duty are keeping with the highest traditions of military service and reflect great credit upon himself, his unit, and the United States Army."

General Walker opened a blue presentation case on his desk and pinned the Silver Star to Jackson's Ike jacket. "Stand fast, MacKenzie." He picked up a second piece of paper. "The Soldier's Medal is hereby awarded to Sergeant Jackson J. MacKenzie, US Army, 1st Cavalry Division, TDY to Easy Company, 2nd Battalion, 27th Infantry Regiment, 25th Infantry Division. For heroic conduct during watch duty for the 25th Infantry Division Camp on 1 August 1952. While maintaining strict adherence to his duty, Sergeant MacKenzie spotted two North Korean officers trying to infiltrate the camp by using a leather cow suit. Due to his vigilance, he captured the two North Korean officers and turned them over to his commanding officer. Those men became a treasure trove of information, giving our intelligence unit the names of their commanding officers and the locations of upcoming operations for asylum in the United States. This information helped greatly in the defense of the Jamestown line. Sergeant MacKenzie's brave actions and adherence to duty helped to maintain our defensive line, thereby reducing casualties and saving lives. His gallant conduct and heroic foresightedness is in keeping with the highest traditions of military service and reflects great credit upon himself, his unit, and the United States Army."

The general removed the Soldier's Medal from a presentation case and pinned it beside the Silver Star. He pulled out one more medal, a Purple Heart bearing an oak leaf cluster, and pinned it next to the other two. "I also present you with the Purple Heart, second award. At ease."

"Yes, sir." Jackson put his hand behind his back. His Ike jacket was getting heavy.

"When you show up on reception day, most of the cadet's jaws will drop upon seeing your salad bowl."

"Yes, sir." He had to agree. The man was his CO and he was right.

General Walker placed the presentation cases and certificate holders in a paper bag with handles.

General Gatlin, Colonel Skinner, Lt. Colonel Barton, and Captain Zeller crowded around him.

General Gatlin shook Jackson's hand. "I hate losing such an excellent soldier. But I look forward to the day when I see you with gold bars on your shoulders. It's been an honor and a pleasure having you under my command. I hope to one day have you there again. Until we meet again, take care of yourself, MacKenzie."

Jackson smiled. "Yes, sir. I will and thank you."

Colonel Skinner, Lt. Colonel Barton, and Captain Zeller shook his hand. They echoed General Gatlin's sentiments. The four men left the room, leaving him alone with General Walker.

General Walker nodded. "Go enjoy your evening. Have a good dinner and relax. Tomorrow, start impressing me all over again."

Jackson came to attention. "Yes, sir. By your leave."

"You're dismissed." General Walker waved at the door. "Go, Trooper, I have work to do."

Jackson turned, exited the open door into the outer office, and left the building. Only his parents being here could make this day even better. He looked at the sky and winked. "Thanks, Dad." He jumped into a waiting jeep and went to his new home, his new unit, the 8th Cavalry.

CHAPTER 7

October 16, 1952
Port of Pohang, South Korea

Jackson shouldered his duffle bag and M1 rifle as he disembarked the amphibious transport. He was tired. *Work his butt* off was right. The division occupied a vast training area of 155,000 acres on Hokkaidō.

Lt. Simmons ran him through drill after drill on dry land. Pushed him hard. He needed hard. That way, he could make up for the lost time. Most of these men survived the first amphibious landing of the Korean War. Here at Pohang on July 18, 1950.

His first attempt at leaving an amphibious transport for the beach on his first live exercise went reasonably well. He did trip over his radioman about one hundred yards in and fell on his face. That was embarrassing, but he brushed it off. The rest of the exercise went by the numbers. Red team beat the blue team defending the beach. Red Ghost Three, his squad, took the command bunker with no casualties. Lt. Simmons bought them a case of beer as a reward. He let his squad have it and drank coffee. Beer just didn't taste good, more like weak piss.

Not only did Lt. Simmons demand perfection in the exercises, he demanded it in physical training as well. Their platoon ran hundreds of miles. Lifted thousands of pounds of weights in the gym and did thousands of sit-ups. Jackson was in the best shape of his life. He resembled a bodybuilder with his rock-hard biceps and six-pack abdomen more than the skinny seventeen-year-old kid at basic training. That was only about eleven months ago. Time really flew by. On his last physical exam upon entry into the 8th Cavalry, he was six feet tall. He'd grown over an inch in Korea. The doctor said he was still growing and would probably push six foot one or taller. He liked that.

A line of deuce-and-a-halves waited for them at the dock. Jackson threw his gear into the back of the closest one. He climbed inside and sat on the bench. His squad, Cpl. Britt, Cpl. Fedderson, PFCs Tucker, Barker, Davis, King, Hill, and Privates Ziegler, Hall, and Rivera came up behind him.

Their destination, Pusan. Their assignment, perform security missions around the cities of Pusan and Taegu. With them so far in the rear, they were not likely to see action unless the North Koreans and Chinese pushed their way south, way past the Jamestown line near the 38th Parallel.

To him, quiet was good. He could use a routine assignment for a while. The one thing he learned over the last few months, war was hell.

October 31, 1952

Jackson leaned back on his bunk. They had the day off. It was 2nd squad's turn at guard duty. What could he do to make it a relaxing day for his men? He glanced at the wall calendar next to the barracks window then realized it was Halloween. That had always been such a fun day with his brother.

Trick-or-treating around base housing was always interesting. Marines, especially those who survived the Pacific campaign, had a wicked sense of humor sometimes. Instead of candy, they gave out things like black shoe polish, empty candy wrappers, cans of C-rations, pencils, bottle caps, and miscellaneous junk. That's what made it a blast. Not knowing. The trick part. That junk was treasure to him and his brother. They could play war with it.

Shoe polish became face paint. They ate the C-rations like grunts in the trenches then filled the cans with mud. Those became grenades they threw at each other. Easy to tell who got hit. Their mother hated it when they came in covered in mud and tracked it around the house. The pencils made bipods for their broomstick rifles. Bottle caps were bullets.

Hmmm. Let's see how creative the guys are. He climbed off his bunk. "Anyone interested in having a contest?"

"What kind of contest?" Cpl. Britt asked.

"A Halloween one. I have a weekend pass already signed by the LT in my locker. The person who comes up with the best costume gets it."

"Who decides?"

"Me. Who's in?"

Shouts of "me" echoed in the barracks.

"Okay." Jackson looked at his watch. "Three hours…Go!"

The men dove into their lockers.

Cpl. Britt, Cpl. Fedderson, PFCs Tucker, Barker, Davis left the barracks. PFCs King, Hill, and Privates Ziegler, Hall, and Rivera soon followed them.

This is going to be fun. Jackson leaned back with his manual. He had some quiet time to read.

Lt. Simmons came in. "What's with the squad?"

Jackson stood. "They are trying to find costumes, sir."

"For what?"

"Halloween. I wanted to get some bonding going, you know, for unit cohesion, so I…offered the pass you gave me to the person with the best costume."

"I commend you for being willing to give it up. But that pass, Sergeant, is for your hard work. You earned it," Simmons said.

"I know, sir. But I wanted the men to have fun. And get something out of it in return."

"You continue to impress me, MacKenzie. Are you taking part in this contest?"

"No, sir. I'm the judge." Jackson smiled inwardly. He did this so much as a child, he wanted his men to enjoy it.

"How about we both judge? I'll authorize another pass for the best costume and you keep yours. You've worked hard to get these men ready for combat. I want you to take a break before you fall on your face from exhaustion. Got it," Lt. Simmons said loudly to emphasize his point.

"If you say so, sir."

"I do. How long did you give them?"

Jackson smiled. "Three hours."

"I'll be back in three hours then." Lt. Simmons left the barracks.

Glad that he liked the idea. Jackson leaned back into his pillows with his Army manual, FM 22-100 Command and Leadership for the Small Unit Leader.

It was one manual of many in the stack on his table. FM 22-10 Leadership, FM 60-5 Amphibious Operations Battalion in Assault Landings, FM 7-10 Infantry Field Manual, Rifle Company, Rifle Regiment, FM 60-10 Amphibious Operations: Regiment in Assault Landings, FM 6-20 Artillery Tactics and Technique, FM 30-5 Combat Intelligence, FM 6-140 The Field Artillery Battery, FM 7-40 Infantry Regiment, FM 22-5 Drill and Ceremonies, FM 21-11 First Aid for Soldiers, FM 21-18 Foot Marches, FM 21-20 Physical Training, FM 6-10 Field Artillery Communications, FM 6-75 105mm Howitzer M2 Series Towed, and FM 7-17 The Armored Infantry Company and Battalion.

Three hours later

One by one, the squad entered the barracks. They grabbed a cup of coffee or wandered around the room.

Jackson waited until everyone had returned. "Line up in front of your bunks."

The men scrambled around until everyone was in the right place.

Lt. Simmons came in and smiled. "Not bad."

Jackson and Lt. Simmons walked down the line, inspecting the men.

Cpl. Britt was wearing a white sheet with eye holes cut out.

"You're a ghost, right, Britt?" Simmons asked.

"Sir, yes, sir," Britt boomed out.

Cpl. Fedderson's face was painted white with red lipstick on his mouth. Around his waist, a piece of camouflage netting.

"What are you, Corporal?" Jackson asked.

"Ballet dancer, Sarge." Fedderson curtsied.

"Is the netting supposed to be a tutu?" Simmons asked.

"Yes, sir."

"Inventive," Jackson replied.

PFC Tucker had a black cloth mask over his eyes, a piece of rope around his waist with a bayonet stuck under it.

Jackson thought for a moment. "Zorro?"

"Yes, Sarge," Tucker said.

PFC Davis was wearing his service cap, aviator sunglasses, and an Army issue trench coat. A stick jammed into half a corncob was stuck between his teeth.

Simmons shook his head. "Do you know, MacKenzie?"

"Sure do. The corncob gives it away. General MacArthur, right, Davis?"

"Yeah, Sarge. Hit it right on the head."

PFC Barker had on shoulder pads and a football helmet from the sports locker. He imitated the Heisman pose with a football in his hand

"Not bad, Barker," Simmons said.

PFC Hill had a black sheet as a cape, white face paint, and red dots next to his lips.

Simmons cocked his head. "Any ideas, MacKenzie?"

"Hmmm…not really. Okay, Hill, what?"

"Vampire, Sarge. Count Dracula," Hill announced proudly.

Simmons nodded. "Now, I see it. Nice use of makeup."

"Yes, sir. I made soap teeth but had to spit them out. Tasted awful."

Jackson and Simmons laughed.

Private Ziegler had on his pack, helmet with his rifle over his shoulder, and a small American flag on a stick in his hand. He placed the flagstick between the floorboards.

Simmons turned to Jackson. "I have no clue."

"I do, sir." His knowledge of the Marine Corps from his father's stories came in handy. "The flag-raising on Iwo Jima, right?"

"You got it, Sarge. My uncle served in the 5th Marine Division."

"Good man." *Might have served under Dad.*

"Those were brave men. I salute them," Simmons said.

Ziegler's chest puffed out even farther. "Thank you, sir."

Private Hall jammed his head down into his collar. He had an orange-painted cabbage with black eyes and a jagged mouth under one arm with a horse bridle slung over his shoulder.

Simmons looked at Jackson then back at Hall. "Hmm…Headless horseman?"

"Yes, sir," Hall said.

Private Rivera held up his hands and waved them around.

"Who are you?" Jackson asked.

"The French in WWII. They surrendered," Rivera said.

Jackson and Simmons looked at each other then burst out laughing with the squad.

Simmons wiped his hand across his face. "Good one, Rivera. Okay, everyone, relax. Come with me, MacKenzie."

Jackson followed Lt. Simmons to the other side of the room.

"What do you think?"

"Let's see." Jackson scratched his chin. "My pick for first place, Davis. I love the corncob."

"I concur. Got a runner-up?"

"Yes, Ziegler."

"Excellent choice. How about honorable mention?"

"Tucker."

"I like that too." Simmons returned to the men. "Okay…the winner is…General MacArthur. Good job, Davis."

PFC Davis stood and bowed. "Thank you, Lieutenant."

"You've got the next one, MacKenzie."

"Got it, sir. Second place goes to…Ziegler." Jackson smiled. "My dad was there too." He wasn't going to give any other information.

"And Ziegler, for the nice tribute, you get a one-day pass," Simmons added.

"Thanks, sir," Ziegler said, placing his helmet on the shelf behind him.

"Honorable mention goes to…Tucker."

"Yes, sir. I loved the book *The Curse of Capistrano*," Tucker said.

Simmons picked up a bag from the floor. "Candy bars from the PX in Seoul. Spread them around. Good job, everyone. You made my day. Consider yourselves off the duty schedule for tomorrow. I'll have Taylor's squad take it. You'll take their patrol on November 2nd."

"Thanks, LT," Jackson said. It would give him more time to read his manuals.

"No. Thank you, MacKenzie. You're turning into one hell of a squad leader. I'm going to send up my recommendation for your promotion to Sergeant First Class."

"Yes, sir. Thank you, sir."

Simmons nodded and left the barracks.

Jackson leaned back in his bunk. He had a lot of reading to do. That would give him even more responsibilities if the brass approved it.

December 7, 1952

The platoon came to a halt in front of the barracks. All they had seen since arriving in Korea was—nothing. No action. Just patrolling around Taegu and Pusan. Peace and quiet like Jackson wanted. To keep them on their toes, Lt. Simmons took them out on a two-day overnight forty-mile ruck march with fifty-pound packs.

"Left face," Lt. Simmons called out.

The platoon faced him.

"Fall out."

Jackson unshouldered his pack and limped into the barracks with his men. He hung his pack and helmet on a wall hook next to his bunk. He was in great shape but all those miles in combat boots carrying an M1, five bandoleers of ammo, and wearing fifty pounds on his back pushed him to the limit. His feet hurt like the dickens. Fire shot up his legs with each step.

Cpl. Britt approached him. "Sergeant, what are your orders?"

"None, other than getting some rack time. We don't have patrol duty until next week." Jackson grabbed his bag holding a towel, change of uniform, and shaving kit then went to the showers. He stripped off his filthy shirt and sat on the bench. Slowly, he removed his boots then noticed his socks were sticky, damp, and stank. Carefully, he peeled off his socks. His feet were covered in lacerated blisters. Inside his boots, crusted, dried blood. *Shit! Should've changed my socks last night. Gotta hide this from the LT. Don't want to wind up on sick call.*

After taking a shower and dressing, he dusted sulfanilamide on the blisters and wrapped his feet in gauze from the latrine first aid kit. For the pain, he took two aspirin then rolled clean socks over the gauze then eased on his boots.

Tonight, he would finish his book, *The Catcher in the Rye* by J. D. Salinger. Not normally something he would read, but it was good. The chaplain loaned it to him. So he had to return it. Reading would keep him off his feet so they could heal.

On his way into the barracks, Jackson heard music turned low. No one in the squad had a radio unless it came in the afternoon mail delivery. They weren't allowed to have radios in the field because they emitted radio waves that could give away their position. In the barracks, it didn't matter. Music was a welcome relief from the boredom of patrol duty. It would help take his mind off his discomfort.

Jackson walked through a toilet paper barrier at the entrance to the squad bay. Confetti made of torn-up bits of newspaper floated down around him.

"Surprise," yelled the men of his squad.

"Huh?"

"Happy birthday, Sarge," Cpl. Britt said.

Jackson thought for a second. All the days had run together. Yesterday was December 6th. How'd he forget his own birthday? "Thanks, guys."

Lt. Simmons handed him a box. "We all chipped in and got this for you."

"Thanks, LT." He opened the box wrapped in the comic section of *Stars and Stripes*. Inside, a set of West Point Black Knight sweats and a thick tan hardcover book. *A Soldier's Story* by General Omar N. Bradley.

"General Walker told me you wanted to go to West Point so I got the sweats shipped over. We bought the book to give you a jump start on your military history."

"Thanks, guys." Jackson thumbed through the book. All 678 pages. It would take him a while. That was a good thing. More time on his back. He looked around. "Who got the radio?"

"Me." Lt. Simmons looked around, a sly grin on his face. "I snagged it from the communications bunker. They won't miss it. You and your men earned a piece of home."

"Yes, sir." Jackson hoped if he became an officer, he'd be as good as Simmons. Right now, he was a total doofus when it came to foot care. *Tomorrow, I'll requisition a new pair of boots and draw more socks from supply.*

December 25, 1952 - Pusan, South Korea

Jackson took a deep breath. Condensation from his exhaled breath hung in the air in front of his face. The snow on the ground didn't lighten his mood. He was cold to his bones. A beating away at his resolve bitter cold.

He'd been with his new unit, the 7th Cavalry Regiment for eleven days after the 8th Regiment rotated back to Hokkaidō, Japan. Now he had a new squad of troopers. Men who'd been through some of the fiercest fighting in Korea. He felt the pressure of making a good first impression.

Slowly, he went into the mess hall. He stomped his numb feet to get the feeling back and remove the snow from his boots.

The room was sparsely decorated with a garland made of faded, multi-colored construction paper rings draped from the ceiling. A small, scraggly pine tree stood in one corner. Home-made ornaments hung from its branches. Roughly carved soap animals, vehicles, and objects made from frag and empty shell casings. A well-used red rope garland encircled the tree. The tinsel was thinly cut old uniform pieces. On top, a star made of brown cardboard and glitter. Underneath, rolls of sandpaper-like toilet paper with twine bows on top. Christmas music played from the overhead speakers.

Jackson picked up a tray and went through the line. This was his first Christmas outside the States. Even in basic training, they made sure Christmas was decent. Good food, a day off, and no drill sergeants on their backs.

The food in the steaming buffet trays looked like dog food or pig slop. Gray-colored spam shaped like a turkey. The mess cook even sliced a piece off as if it was real. The runny mashed potatoes were covered in watery brown gravy. The chewy roll bounced when it hit the plate. Semi-green beans and mushy carrots rounded out the meal. For dessert, bright-orange colored pumpkin-flavored pie in a burnt crust.

Jackson carried his food to an empty table, sat down, and tried the so-called turkey. It tasted like a salt lick soaked in the nasty kimchi buried everywhere. "Yuk." He spit it back on the plate. Next, he tried the mashed potatoes. At least, they tasted like potatoes. So did the green beans and carrots. Then he ate the pie. It was sweet, almost too sweet, but better than the gray-colored meat substance.

Cpl. Pagano, his buddy from the 25th Infantry and a recent transfer to the 7th Cavalry Regiment, set his tray on the table and sat down next to Jackson.

"Hey, Kyle."

"Hey, JJ. Any plans since we don't have watch duty tonight?"

"Yeah, read, and go to bed." He just got a new book. *Indian Paint* by Glenn Balch.

"Not going to the movie?"

"No, seen it already." Jackson had no desire to see *Singin' in the Rain* for the fourth time in a month. "Did you get anything from home?"

Kyle smiled. "Yeah, Mom sent me a nice, thick wool stocking cap. It's much warmer than my army one. She also sent a bagful of hard candy, candy bars, gum, and taffy."

"I'll trade you two packs of cigarettes from my rations for the candy bars and gum." Jackson pushed his tray aside. He didn't need to lug those nasty things around in his pack.

"Deal." Kyle slapped Jackson's open palm.

Jackson sniffed. "Thanks."

"What's wrong?"

"First Christmas alone."

"Oh, yeah. I forgot about your parents. Did you get anything?"

"No. Guess it got lost in the mail." Jackson knew Uncle Manny and Aunt Sara sent something. But the Army was famous for losing packages with good stuff in them.

"Maybe it'll get here soon."

"But not today." He was sad, not because he didn't get a Christmas present. His one Christmas wish, his beloved mom and dad would return. It was an empty one but the only thing he truly wanted. Presents were things. Objects. They could be replaced. Nothing could replace his parents.

Kyle gripped his shoulder. "I'm going to the movie. The candy bars are in the box under my bunk. Help yourself."

"I'll put the cigarettes in the box."

"See you later." Kyle left the mess hall.

Jackson flipped up the collar of his field jacket to protect his ears and went outside. He shoved his hand in his pockets and headed for the barracks.

The snow crunched as he walked along the path. Around him, the air was still. Bitter cold. A light freezing fog hung low across the compound. It swirled as he walked through it.

His first stop in the barracks, Kyle's bunk. He pulled out the candy bars and gum then replaced them with the cigarettes from his coat pocket. Those trading items he always kept with him. You never knew when a good barter opportunity would pop up.

As the squad sergeant, he had his own room at the far end of the barracks. When he opened the door, on top of his bunk sat a large cardboard box. He pulled off the note taped to the top. Before he read it, he checked the return address. Sara Malone, Double M Ranch, Beaver Creek, MT. The one thing he wondered, how did it get here? No mail delivery on a holiday.

Jackson sat on his bunk and read the note.

05 December 1952

Jackson,

I had this shipped to the 1st Marine Division. Knowing the mail service, I wanted to make sure it got to you in time. I instructed Colonel Reddington to have it hand-delivered to you in Pusan. This is your first Christmas far from home. I wanted you to feel loved. I know you miss your mom and dad. We do too. I've also been in your shoes and know how lonely it can get during the holidays in a war zone. I sent Jim a care package to Annapolis. But not as much. He lives in a nice, warm dormitory, eating hot meals and having quiet nights. You're in cold ass Korea, eating mess hall food and wondering when the next attack will come your way. If you will live or die from day to day. Take care of yourself.

P.S. Sara says to keep your head down. Count on having all of your favorites to eat the next time you are at the ranch.

Merry Christmas, kid. We love you.
Mangus and Sara Malone

Jackson smiled and wiped away a tear. At least he got a small slice of home. He slit the tape with his pocket knife. One that his father gave him for his fourteenth birthday. A stainless steel four-bladed Kingston, U.S. Marine Corps stamped on the side. The same one his father carried during the Pacific campaign. Inside the box, a Christmas card signed by Mangus and Sara, thick long johns, a wool stocking hat, wool socks, underwear, t-shirts, four rolls of soft toilet paper, a bag of candy bars, and another box.

First, he sniffed it. Sweet, chocolate, vanilla. He knew that smell and ripped open the box. It was filled with Sara's home-baked chocolate chip cookies. He ate one. Somewhat crumbly after the long trip from the states but delicious. Unable to stop, he ate six more. They were that good.

Thirsty, he went into the squad bay and poured a cup of the ever-present coffee from the stainless steel percolator on the wood stove that heated the barracks. He stoked the fire with fresh wood, took his cup into his room, and shut the door.

Jackson placed his new clothing in his footlocker. He removed his coat, uniform, and boots then put on his sweats. The cookie box he set on the shelf next to his bunk with his coffee cup. They might not last through the evening as he settled back with his book. He needed that, needed to feel loved. To feel like someone cared about him far away from home.

CHAPTER 8

February 12, 1953 – Port of Pohang, South Korea

Jackson waited at the dock with the trucks picking up the 5th Cavalry Regiment. His new unit. The 7th was rotating back to Hokkaidō, Japan. General Walker wanted to keep him in Korea for some reason. He didn't know why. All he knew, he was in 1st Platoon, Mike Company, 3rd Battalion under Lt. Clark. He had to get to know a new squad of men. Again.

Except for Cpl. Pagano. He was also transferred into the 5th Regiment. Jackson sent a request up the chain of command for Pagano's assignment as his assistant squad leader. A request quickly approved at headquarters.

The one piece of information that came his way through the underground Army grapevine. He was staying in Pusan, not going to Koje-do. That was good. He didn't want POW camp duty. After seeing what truly happens in war—death and destruction—he might say or do something he shouldn't to mouthy North Koreans and Chinese soldiers. They murdered his parents. He didn't want to kill his dream of being an officer or wind up in prison.

Bored, he climbed onto the hood, shaded his eyes with his hand, and looked around. The men were disembarking the amphibious transport with their gear.

A young man wearing silver lieutenant's bars approached the truck. "You MacKenzie?"

Jackson jumped down and came to attention. "Yes, sir."

"I'm Lieutenant Clark. At ease. Heard a lot of good things about you."

"Thank you, sir. Want me to get your gear?"

Lt. Clark shook his head. "No, I'll get it. I don't expect you to be my porter."

"Yes, sir."

"MacKenzie, under my command, if you feel the need to voice your opinion or point out something I missed, do it. The scoop on you is you're one of the best soldiers in the unit. And smart as a whip. I want to know if you see something I don't. Got it?"

"Yes, sir."

"Good." The lieutenant threw his gear into the back of the truck and climbed in the cab.

Jackson smiled. *I've got a reputation to maintain. Hope I don't screw my chances of going to West Point.*

March 26, 1953

Cold. Rain. Snow. Ice. Heat. Humidity. Baking sun. Korea had every extreme of weather. Sometimes in a single day. All within hours. Just wait five minutes and the weather would change. Sometimes for the better. Most of the time, for the worse, with him in the middle of it.

Jackson slogged through the mud with his patrol in the woods outside of Pusan. He was wet and cold from the top of his head to his toes. Mud coated everything. Him, his pack, his rifle. It was even in his underwear, chafing his groin. The inside of his legs were raw. The rain poncho did nothing except funnel the water down his collar as it dripped off his helmet.

Cpl. Pagano ran up. He stopped and slid onto his butt.

"Nice landing, Pagano." Jackson laughed.

Pagano stood, slinging mud from his hands. "Yeah."

"Anything to report."

"Nothing. Not a soul around. Didn't even see a fish." Pagano wiggled his hand like a fin.

"Funny. Okay, gather up the squad. Let's head in. It's 2nd squad's turn to go swimming."

"You got that right." Pagano grabbed the other men dotted along the trail. They fell in behind him.

Jackson headed toward the camp. He was ready for a hot shower to thaw out and a hot meal. The general hadn't contacted him about his application to West Point. That could only mean one thing. He didn't get selected. One thing did help his mood. He had one month, one day, and a wake-up to go then he was leaving this God-forsaken country. Hopefully forever.

April 15, 1953

Jackson led his men around the outside of the small village. Third Squad was overdue in returning from patrol. Their last know location, this village, San-Seong.

Corporal Pagano came up to his side, M1 rifle at the ready. "No movement at all, Sarge."

"Nothing?" Jackson took off his helmet, wiped his forehead with his sleeve then put the helmet back on.

"Didn't even see a chicken?"

"Hmmm…" Jackson pulled out his binoculars and scanned the area. He couldn't spot anything either. Not even smoke from cooking fires. He sniffed to make sure. All he could detect, the smells of Korea. Kimchee, mud, fetid water, and…he took a deeper breath through his nose. The odor was faint but there. Decay, decomposition of something that used to be alive. Might be rotting plants but he didn't think so. Too rancid, too putrid, too dead.

"Corporal, I have a bad feeling about this."

Pagano nodded. "Me too."

Jackson turned around. "All right, we go in. Stay frosty. Heads on a swivel. Two men check every hut. No one goes into any structure alone. Got it?"

Replies of "Yeah, Sarge," came from his squad.

"Move out." Jackson waved the men forward on the dirt road, more of a narrow footpath.

They moved slowly into the village. At first, nothing appeared. Just tall grass, trees, tipped donkey carts with the shaft poles pointed up. The smell, however, got stronger. At the first hut, Pagano and McCoy peeled off and went inside. The squad kept moving. Galindez and Zito checked the next hut.

In the center of the village was a well surrounded by a stone wall. Around it, dozens of distended, bloated human bodies of every shape and size. Even the animals, goats, chickens, horses, cows, and donkeys lay scattered around them. All dead.

His men sucked in rapid breaths. He heard mumbles of "Oh, shit! Our father who art in heaven…" "Damn!" "Bastards." "Filthy gooks."

A shiver went down Jackson's spine. Today's lunch of franks and beans rolled around in his stomach, threatening to reappear. His gut feeling was proving true. And way too close to home.

As they moved closer, the smell went from bearable to nauseatingly pungent. Jackson pulled out a handkerchief and tied it around his nose and mouth. It helped a little, if he breathed shallow and slow. The scene made him want to suck in air like he was running a marathon. He used all of his willpower to keep from hyperventilating, wishing for a dab of mentholatum rub under his nostrils to cut the smell.

Thousands of flies flew in a thick, billowing cloud around the well. The bodies were black with them. They seemed to move as if alive.

Jackson waved his rifle over the first body to remove some of the flies. Darkened green fatigues peppered with holes and sergeant stripes on the sleeves appeared. Fields, the leader of 3rd Squad. "Shit!" *Our job was to find them. Save them. Bring them home.* Shock, horror, and sadness washed over him. He heaved up his lunch, spit the taste out, and turned away. Fields' wife and kids should never see this. And he sure didn't want to. It would be ingrained in his memory for the rest of his life.

Pagano ran up. His eyes were flashing with fear, disgust, and anger. "Sarge, everyone in the village is dead. We found all of 3rd Squad."

What the fuck happened here? How'd the gooks get the drop on them? "Yeah. Have Galindez and Zito get two bonfires going. We'll burn the bodies of the villagers and animals so the scavengers don't get them. Radio!"

PFC Hunt ran up. "Yes, Sarge."

Jackson shoved his emotions into a little box. He couldn't afford to feel right now. His contempt for anything North Korean might make him do something stupid. Duty came first—grieving and anger came later, in private. He yanked the handset off Hunt's radio pack and keyed it up. "Casper one-two to Casper one-six."

"This is one-six, go ahead."

"Found 3rd Squad. No survivors. Looks like the gooks executed the entire village along with them. Including the animals. Request helicopters or trucks to pick up the bodies."

"Acknowledged one-two. Expect two more squads as reinforcements soon. You know what to do. Out."

Jackson gave the handset to PFC Hunt. He took off his pack and pulled out his poncho liner. It would do until someone arrived with body bags. Fighting his queasy stomach, he pulled Fields' body onto the poncho liner and wrapped the ends over him. *What did this simple village do to deserve this? It had no strategic value. Just a spot in the middle of nowhere. Do I really want to see dead men, women, and babies all the time? Should I tell General Walker to pull my West Point application and go home to a normal life? So I won't see death and carnage at every turn.*

April 27, 1953

Jackson packed his gear in his duffle bag. Today was his last day in Korea. He was beyond ready to go stateside. Back to the world. Alone. He had no real home to return to. That house belonged to the Marine Corps. The

Army was his only home now. Maybe. His enlistment was over in December.

Cpl. Pagano handed him a piece of paper. He was headed home in two days. "This is my address and phone number in Wisconsin. Don't be a stranger. Give me a call."

"I will." Jackson tucked the paper into his pocket. I haven't heard from General Walker. Guess I didn't get selected."

"I'm so sorry, JJ. I know how much that meant to you. What are you going to do?"

"Use the only option I have left. Go work on Uncle Manny's ranch."

Lt. Clark entered the barracks. "MacKenzie."

Jackson came to attention. "Yes, sir."

"Report to General Walker's office tomorrow at 1200 for your out brief. A transport is leaving from the airfield at 2100 tonight for Chitose Air Base. Be on it."

"Yes, sir." *Wonder what that's about. I already had my out brief with Captain Heller. Guess the general wants to tell me personally I didn't get into the academy.*

April 28, 1953 - Chitose Air Base, Hokkaidō, Japan

Jackson sat on the bench outside of General Walker's office in his service dress uniform. He adjusted his tie, running his hand down the blade to straighten it.

At 1200 hours, First Sergeant Katz opened the inner door. "He's ready for you, Sergeant."

Jackson nodded, marched into the office, and came to attention. "Sergeant MacKenzie reporting as ordered, sir."

"At ease, MacKenzie, sit down."

"Yes, sir." Jackson sat in the chair in front of the desk.

General Walker sat on the edge of the desk. "I have something for you." He held out a Combat Infantryman Badge and two gold overseas service bars.

Jackson accepted the items then rubbed his thumb across the bar's stitched surface. "That's why you kept me in country."

"Yes. So you can wear those on your sleeve." General Walker pointed at the stack of blue presentation cases on his desk. "Those are your Korean Service Medal, United Nations Korea Medal, the new National Defense Service Medal, and the Republic of Korea Presidential Unit Citation. I figured you wouldn't want me to make a big deal out of it this time."

"Thank you, sir."

"Don't thank me just yet." General Walker handed him an envelope.

On the front, stamped in the upper left corner, United States Military Academy, West Point, New York. Jackson's heart beat faster. He carefully opened the envelope, hoping it wasn't a rejection letter.

HEADQUARTERS
DEPARTMENT OF THE ARMY
OFFICE OF THE ADJUTANT GENERAL
WASHINGTON 25, DC

IN REPLY REFER TO

AGPB-M 201 MacKenzie, Jackson J   22 April 1953
(22 April 53)

Sergeant Jackson J. MacKenzie
US Army - 1st Cavalry Division
Hokkaidō, Japan

Sergeant MacKenzie,

You have been selected for admission and are authorized to report to the United States Military Academy (USMA) West Point, New York, on 7 July 1953, before 10 A.M., Daylight Savings Time. You will find helpful information in the enclosed instructions about transportation, baggage, funds, and other matters pertaining to admission.

You are to be congratulated on this opportunity for admission to the Military Academy, for it comes only to a select few of America's youth. It presents a challenge that will demand your best effort. Therefore, it is suggested that you give serious thought to your desire for a military career, as without proper motivation, you may find it difficult to conform to what may be a new way of life.

Wishing you a full measure of success and satisfaction as a member of the Corps of Cadets and later a commissioned officer in the Armed Forces of our country, I am

Sincerely yours,

C. N. Lambert

Enclosures

C. N. Lambert
Major General, USA
The Adjutant General

Jackson reread the letter to make sure he wasn't hallucinating. Maybe he'd died and gone to heaven. His heart beat so rapidly it felt like it would explode from his chest. He drew slow breaths to keep from hyperventilating, then looked up at the general. "I made it?"

General Walker held out his hand. "Yes, you did. Your near-perfect scores on the achievement tests impressed a lot of people. Puts you in the top one percent of your class. Congratulations."

Jackson accepted the handshake. He was still in shock even though the general had said months earlier that he was sure to get accepted. Things were never a given until they happened. And it did. He wasn't so sure yesterday. In fact, he'd resigned himself that he was headed home to an unknown future. "What now, sir?"

"Now, you go home. You have forty days leave on the books. From today until your flight stateside in two days, you're attached to the headquarters battalion. Relax and enjoy the time off. Go to the NCO club. Get a good meal. Drink a few beers. Take in a movie or two. Sleep. Things will get hectic once you get home. At Fort Hood, they'll take care of your paperwork then send your service record book and transfer orders to West Point. Once that is taken care of, you'll be on leave until your report date. I suggest you go see your godfather and take care of your family business."

"Yeah, I need to pack up the house at Camp Pendleton. General Malone couldn't bring himself to do it. He feels so responsible for dad's death and Jim's been too busy with his classes at Annapolis."

"So it falls on you."

"Yeah, and it'll be hard." Jackson stood and held out his hand. "Thank you so much for your support, sir."

General Walker shook his hand. "The honor was mine. It's rare to find someone like you, MacKenzie. You're a diamond in the rough. You'll shine as one of our best and brightest once the academy takes the sharp edges off. Good luck, Trooper."

Jackson came to attention. "By your leave, sir."

"Dismissed."

"Yes, sir." Jackson grabbed the bag in which the general had placed all his awards and paperwork then left the office. He had to call Uncle Manny and tell him the good news. Next, he had to call Jim. His brother would be so proud of him. He stayed the course, toed the line, and grabbed the brass ring at the end. He sure hoped his mom and dad were watching from above and smiling. Their memory kept him going.

CHAPTER 9

May 1, 1953
20,000 feet over the Pacific Ocean

Tired of doing nothing, Jackson unlatched his seatbelt and stood. He stretched and looked over the full cargo pallets. Most of the men seated around him were asleep. At their feet, packs, duffle bags, helmets, and M1 rifles. On their shoulders, a variety of different unit patches. The 1st Cavalry Division, the 25th Infantry Division, the 45th Infantry Division, and the 40th Infantry Division. Dotted among them, a few Marines, Air Force, and Sailors. Their heads were leaning forward, back, or to the side. Some snoring. A few with their mouths open, drool running down their chins. All returning to the states. The war was over for them. For the time being, at least.

Instead of sitting down, he explored the plane and used the facilities. A cargo pallet with an attached plastic port-a-potty. The stench almost made him puke. It was full and not just with human waste. The smell of vomit mixed with alcohol was unmistakable.

Under his feet, he felt the vibrations of the four propeller-driven piston engines. Curious, he went to the front of the plane. Next to the cockpit door sat an enlisted man in a green flight suit, the loadmaster.

"Sergeant, can I look at the cockpit?" Jackson asked.

The airman, a staff sergeant, cocked his head in curiosity. "Sure, why not? We don't get many curious grunts. Hang on a minute, let me ask the captain."

"Thanks."

The staff sergeant knocked on the cockpit door and went inside. He returned a minute later. "Captain Fisher said it's okay." He pointed at the open door. "Go on in."

Jackson stuck his head into the cockpit. The bulkheads were covered with all kinds of lights, switches, and knobs. He went in and stopped. On his right sat a man next to a panel with pull knobs, handles, and gauges. *Flight engineer?* On his left, a man at a desk with a pencil sharpener attached and what looked like a radio setup. *Might be the navigator.* The view through the windows took his breath away. Clouds streamed by quickly and the sky was so blue. Vivid. Bright. Clear. Much bluer than on the ground. He heard the wind roaring over the cockpit windows.

The co-pilot in the right seat stood. "Sit here, Sergeant. See what you think. I've got to hit the head."

"You sure, sir?" Jackson asked. Not positive if the man was joking or not. He didn't want to do something wrong.

"Yeah, I'm sure, or I wouldn't have said it." The co-pilot smiled then left.

Jackson stood still for a second, unsure about everything.

The pilot in the left seat took one hand off the yoke and pointed. "Go ahead. Sit."

"Yes, sir." Jackson climbed into the right seat. Between him and the pilot was a console containing all kinds of controls. He made sure not to touch anything. The last thing he wanted was to make them crash. That would put a damper on an otherwise perfect flight.

The pilot turned his head. "I'm Captain Fisher. You have quite a special salad bowl on that dress uniform, Sergeant."

"Yes, sir," Jackson said, feeling the heat rise up to his ears. He didn't feel like a hero, only a survivor.

"I see the DSC, Silver Star, Soldier's Medal, CIB, Airborne wings, and the Purple Heart in addition to the service ribbons. That's a lot of action. How are you holding up?"

"I'm glad it's over for a while, sir." *Never expected to see that much death.*

"Are you checking out? Heading back to the land of a normal 9 to 5?"

"No, sir. Once I get my paperwork done at Fort Hood and a few weeks of leave, I'm heading to West Point. I'm a plebe in the next class."

"Congratulations."

"Thank you, sir."

"Want to give it a try?"

Jackson looked at Captain Fisher, confused. "Give what a try?"

The captain pointed at the yoke. "This. Fly the plane."

Did he really say that? "Yes, sir...I mean if it's okay with you, sir."

"It's more than okay." Fisher laughed. "I asked you, remember."

"What do I do?"

The captain tapped the yoke in front of him. "Grab this and put your feet on the pedals."

"Okay," Jackson said hesitantly. He did as instructed. Under his hands, the plane moved, more than the vibrations of the engines. It felt alive. Like a bird ready to be released. The pedals pushed against his feet. He tried to keep them in the same place. It wasn't easy, but he managed it. To say he was nervous and unsure was an understatement. This was a 185,000-

pound aircraft that was 48 feet high, 130 feet long with a wingspan of 174 feet flying over the Pacific Ocean. Nothing but water under them. Not a speck of land in sight. And him with no knowledge, experience, or training guiding it.

Captain Fisher took his hands off the yoke. "She's all yours. Just hold her straight and level."

Jackson concentrated on doing that. The plane wanted to do its own thing. He felt it try to go nose down against his arms and pulled back on the yoke.

The captain pointed at a round gauge in front of them, blue on top, black on the bottom. A small silhouette of an airplane sat in the middle. "This is your artificial horizon. It helps you keep the plane level. Keep it on the white line in the center."

Jackson nodded. It took all his concentration to keep them level. The plane felt like a bucking bronco under his hands and feet. A wild animal determined to be set free. He detected the crosswind across the nose through the yoke. To keep them straight, he had to maintain a slight right turn on the controls.

Fisher pointed at another gauge. This one had a small white plane on a black background. Under the plane, a ball rolled inside a curved glass tube. "This is the turn-and-slip indicator. It indicates rotation on the longitudinal, roll, or X-axis. That's an imaginary line drawn through the center of the plane from tail to nose in the normal direction of flight."

"Okay. What are the others?"

"The vertical or Z-axis is up and down. The lateral, pitch, or Y-axis is from side to side."

"Got it." Jackson pictured in his head what the plane was doing. Soaking in the information like a sponge. Maintaining right tension on the yoke would keep them on course. He felt like a race car driver behind the wheel of an Indy 500 car. His heart and brain were going a million miles a second.

"That's the heading indicator or directional gyro." Fisher pointed at a round gauge with N, S, E, W, written on it with numbers and white lines in between. "Keep it on the bearing of one-zero-five. Each line is five degrees."

"Yes, sir."

"This is the altimeter. Keep us around 20,000 feet. That's our cruising altitude."

Jackson glanced at the numbers on the gauge. They were meant to roll. The number, 20,001, kept inching incrementally toward 20,002. He pushed down on the yoke slightly. The roll stopped and steadied at 20,001.

This is the airspeed indicator." Fisher pointed at a round black dial with white numbers on its circumference. "Our cruising speed is 200 miles per hour or 174 knots. I don't have to explain a magnetic compass to a grunt, right?"

"No, sir. Used one many times." *Saved my life and the lives of my men on more than one occasion.*

"Just keep us level and the airspeed steady. You're doing fine." Simmons adjusted a couple of levers in the center console.

"Better than fine," someone said behind them.

Jackson glanced over his shoulder at the co-pilot. "Want me to leave, sir?" *Don't really want to.*

"No, I'm still taking a break. Just keep doing what you're doing, Sergeant." The lieutenant drank from a canteen and ate a cracker. "You've got a steady hand."

"Yes, sir." *Not really. It's taking all I have to control the plane.* Jackson concentrated on the instruments, holding onto the yoke and keeping the pedals in the same position. The aircraft had a life of its own. Air pockets made it jump up and down. The numbers on the altimeter went with it. He managed to keep them steady, around 20,000. Sweat rolled down his face. His heart beat so fast, his chest hurt. He forced himself to breathe normally and not hyperventilate. It was nerve-wracking, holding their lives in his hands. But it was also fun. More than he could have ever imagined. Adrenaline pumped into his system, he felt on top of the world. Euphoric. Invincible. Flying like Superman.

He lost track of how long he sat at the controls. Minutes passed as he stared out the windows and at the instruments. Making sure to follow Captain Fisher's instructions to the letter.

Someone tapped him on the shoulder. "My turn."

Jackson looked up at the lieutenant. "Yes, sir." He made sure Captain Fisher had control then released his death grip on the yoke and climbed out of the seat.

The lieutenant took his place. He picked up a clipboard, made marks on it then hung it on the hook beside his leg.

Jackson wiped his sweaty palms on his pants. As he turned to leave, the captain placed a hand on his arm, bringing him to a stop. "Yes, sir."

"Lieutenant Parsons is correct. You have a natural ability. Too bad you're going to West Point. You'd be a great addition to the Air Force as a pilot."

"Yes, sir. I'd like that. But I have always wanted to be an Infantryman like my dad."

"Was he in the Army too?"

"No, sir. Marine Corps. I may take flying lessons sometime. When I get the chance and have the money." *That might be a while. Don't make much as a cadet or a Second Lieutenant.*

"Got the bug, did you?"

"Yes, sir. Big time. I had a blast. Thank you."

"You're welcome. You served this country with courage, honor, and distinction. We don't get too many of the kids who fly back with us ask to come up here. We figured, why not? It never hurts to let someone dream. To see what they're missing. Maybe give them a direction they didn't think about taking."

Jackson smiled. "No, sir, it doesn't. Thank you again."

"We'll be landing soon, son. Go strap in and...when you do learn to fly, add two hours in your logbook for a C-124 Globemaster II. Just let me know and I'll sign off on it. Understood?"

"Copy that, sir. Understood." Jackson nodded and returned to his seat. The men had woken up. Several of them looked at him funny when he sat down and latched his seat belt. *Let them wonder where I've been.*

The landing wasn't smooth, the heavy cargo plane bounced on its wheels. But it wasn't rough either. As many times as he had flown on these planes in the last year, that was normal for Old Shakey.

When he walked down the cargo ramp, Jackson knelt and touched the tarmac then looked at the sky. *Miss you, Mom and Dad.* He was back in the United States. His country. His home. Alone but alive. No bands, kisses, flowers, or parades like after WWII. Just a day like any other.

One more flight from Norton Air Force Base in San Bernardino, California, to Fort Hood. There this journey would end and another begin. Hopefully, to point him in a direction for the rest of his life.

CHAPTER 10

May 14, 1953
USMC Camp Pendleton, California

Jackson unlocked the front door and entered their old house. It wasn't his home. Not anymore. The tan two-story stucco building was just a shell with four outer walls and a ceiling waiting for the next occupants to move in once he cleaned it out.

He leaned his duffle bag against the wall in the entry hall, took off his Ike jacket, and hung it on the coatrack. After he loosened his tie, he slowly walked around the house. Dust covered everything. The place smelled musty and old, not the clean smell of bleach he remembered. His mother was a meticulous housekeeper. The floors so clean you could eat off them. Never a speck of dust anywhere. A habit she instilled in her children.

His dad tended to leave that cleanliness and order at the office. Muddy boots in the living room. Clothes hung on the furniture. Damp towels on the bathroom floor. Mom hated it. Jackson wished to have those times back. To be a kid again back when everything was so much simpler. Playing with his brother. Following his father around the camp. Asking him questions about everything he did for the men under his command. Listening to his lectures and war stories. Watching him give orders. Trying to emulate everything about him. No worries. Only hopes and dreams for the future.

Jackson changed into his West Point sweats in the living room to keep from getting his service dress uniform dirty. He went upstairs and leaned against the doorjamb of his parents' room. The bed was made. The bedspread was so tight you could bounce a quarter off it. Marine Corps perfect. The dresser was neat. A brush, comb, and bottle of his mother's favorite perfume, Miss Dior, sat on a silver tray. He went over, picked up the bottle, and sniffed. It smelled like his mother. Sweet, floral, spicy, woody, earthy, fresh.

Trying to hold in his emotions, he checked the bathroom. On the vanity was a Gillette safety razor next to a bottle of Old Spice. That was the only aftershave his father ever used. Even though no one had been in this bathroom in almost two years, the scent of Old Spice mixed with Miss Dior still lingered.

He made his way over to the closet. Inside were his father's uniforms. Green fatigues, a Service A green uniform, and his Marine Corps dress blues still in the plastic wrapper from the cleaners. Next to them, his mother's dresses, pants, blouses, and...her old US Army dress uniform from when she was a nurse before WWII. Captain's bars on the shoulders.

Jackson removed that uniform and his father's dress blues. He sat on the bed with them. Holding them. Clutching them against his chest. The memories threatened to overwhelm him. He fought against the tears until he remembered his godfather's poignant words. Crying didn't make you any less of a man. At that point, the floodgates opened, and he openly wept. He missed them so much. Even though he had realized his dream of going to West Point, it didn't feel right. He wasn't whole without them here with him. To witness all he would accomplish. They were the inspiration for his dreams. They should be here. But now his life had been turned upside down. He felt so alone with his brother almost three thousand miles away.

Everything came to a stop. He didn't know how much time had passed until he looked at his watch. Two hours. Slowly, he stood and carefully laid the uniforms on the bed. He wiped at the dried tears with his handkerchief.

Unable to take tackling this room at the moment, he moved on to his. That was easier. He packed his old clothes first. The jeans didn't fit in the waist or the length, and his shirts were all too small. He'd grown in the last year. Now he was six-foot-one instead of the five-foot-eleven skinny kid who enlisted in the Army and nearly thirty pounds heavier. All muscle.

He moved on to his toys, trophies, and stuff. All placed in boxes, padded with old crumpled up newspapers. His baseball mitt went on top after he put it on and slammed his fist into the pocket a couple of times. The leather smelled wonderful. Full of memories. He took this mitt to the baseball game on his last day with his father at home. He and his brother ate until they were stuffed. Hot dogs, popcorn, peanuts, potato chips. Dad let them have anything they wanted. He even caught a foul ball. It still sat on his dresser. What he remembered most, the root beer float at the A & W drive-in. He took off the mitt, stuck the ball in the webbing, placed it in the box, and taped it closed.

"Are you okay?" asked a male voice.

Jackson looked at his godfather standing in the doorway. "Yeah. Thought the 1st Marine Division was still in Korea."

"They are. I was promoted last week to Lieutenant General, confirmed by Congress, and given command of the 1st Marine Expeditionary Force. I wanted to surprise you."

"Really? Congratulations. Did Uncle Jason come home with you?"

"Yes, but he's TAD to Parris Island as a senior drill instructor in the 2nd Training Battalion for the next two months."

He'll love yelling at the new recruits. "I'm glad he's home. Away from the fighting and that rotten hellhole." He couldn't get the nasty stench of death, mud, and kimchi out of his nose.

"Me too. I know this is hard. Do you want some help?"

"Can you take care of Mom and Dad's room? I can't do it right now."

"Sure." Mangus sniffed. Moisture appeared in the corners of his eyes. He quickly wiped it away with his hand.

"Uncle Manny, if you can't, I'll take care of it later." He didn't want to upset his godfather.

"No, I'll do it. Might help me with my feelings of guilt."

"About what?"

"I'm here. James and Kim aren't. You boys are alone now."

"True...but if you were gone, Aunt Sara, Richard, Carrie, and Maxwell would be hurting, and I would be too."

Mangus gave him a sad lop-sided sad smile. "Thanks. You don't know how special you truly are." He disappeared from the door.

Jackson heard thunks down the hall. His godfather was busy in the other room. He stacked the boxes next to the door then moved to his brother's room. Since Jim took most of his personal stuff to Annapolis, boxing up his room went quickly. Old clothes, a few toys, and sports gear. His brother was an athlete. He lettered in baseball, football, and wrestling in high school. This year, he was a varsity wrestler for Navy.

Someone knocked on the front door.

Jackson went downstairs and opened it. Four Marines in fatigues wearing sergeant stripes stood on the porch.

Mangus joined him. "I asked my aide to send some men over to help with the furniture. That is, if you don't mind?"

"No, I appreciate the help." *I'd rather someone do it. Too many memories.* The forts made from the dining room chairs with his mom's bedsheets. The sleepovers with his friends on the living room floor playing board games, eating popcorn, and listening to the radio. Vanilla milkshakes made in the kitchen blender. Wrestling with Jim in the entry hall. Falling asleep on the couch smelling wood smoke from the fireplace. Roasting marshmallows over the open flames on sharpened sticks. The aroma of his father's cigars in the study as he sat at the desk doing his homework.

"Sergeant Gregory, did you get a truck?" Mangus asked.

One of the men nodded. "Yes, sir. I have the keys to a large storage locker too. Compliments of the 1st Marines."

"Thanks, guys," Jackson said. Now he had a place to put everything.

The men came inside. As they took the furniture and beds out of the house, Jackson packed up the kitchen and dining room. He carefully wrapped his mom's favorite china in newspapers to prevent them from breaking. The silverware he placed in a shoebox. Her vacation collection of thimbles and spoons, along with the wooden case, he padded with the linen napkins in another box. Every item had memories. He couldn't let them get damaged in any way. They were his reminder of his mother. An angel to everyone she met. Always willing to lend a helping hand or a simple hug at just the right moment.

Once everything was placed in the truck, Jackson went to each empty room. At the kitchen door, he ran his hand across the marks on the doorframe where his mom recorded their heights with dates and ages. In the living room, he smiled at the small dent still visible where Jim ran his head into the wall while they wrestled. His bedroom walls had pinholes where he hung all his blue ribbons from the riding competitions. Jim's room had a body-shaped impression in the hardwood from his sweat doing sit-ups with his feet hooked under the bed frame. The last stop on his farewell tour, his parents' room. He could still smell Miss Dior and Old Spice.

Mangus placed a hand on Jackson's shoulder. "Ready to go?"

Jackson nodded. "Yeah."

"Let's go to my quarters and take a shower. Then I'll treat you to a steak dinner at the officer's club. I want everyone to see my hero godson wearing one hell of a fruit salad on his Army uniform. James and Kim would be so proud of the man you've become."

"I wish they were here."

"So do I, kid. So do I. By the way, you're staying with me until you have to report to West Point. No arguments. That an order. And I'm taking you to New York. I promise not to go on campus."

"Yes, sir." That was so Uncle Manny.

"Huh? You know better."

"Yes…Uncle Manny." *Oops. Better watch that.*

May 15, 1953

Jackson wanted to keep the 1940 Studebaker Champion left to him in his father's will. Jim got the newer Chevy truck. But he couldn't. No place for the car at West Point, and he couldn't afford the maintenance, insurance, and gas. The payout from his parent's life insurance policies through the NSLI program, $10,000 each, went equally into a trust fund for him and Jim, awarded on their 21st birthdays.

Arguing with the salesman at the car lot would take too long. Time he didn't have. He needed the money to rent a safe deposit box. All his Army paychecks went for his living expenses and travel to West Point. He was going to pay his way whether Uncle Manny liked it or not.

His parent's medals, dog tags, wedding rings, and other cherished items he couldn't take with him. It was against the rules and he didn't want them to wind up missing if a cadet had sticky fingers.

"Have you made up your mind, kid?" the salesman asked.

Kid? Yeah, guess I am. I don't think of myself that way anymore. "Yeah, deal."

"Sign here." The salesman pointed at a line at the bottom of the page.

No going back now. Jackson signed his name.

The salesman tore off the back copy of the contract and handed it to him with the money.

Jackson counted the bills. Three hundred dollars. A lot of money. Not what the car was worth. His dad kept it in mint condition. It looked brand new. Shining in the bright sunlight like black granite outside the building. As he exited, he looked at the car one more time to burn it into his memory.

He caught a bus to the National Bank of San Diego. The way his civilian clothing, jeans, sneakers, t-shirt, and a button-up shirt hung on his body felt weird but comfortable. *Guess I've been in fatigues too long.*

The trip took forever in the lunch hour traffic. Jackson watched the scenery go by. People walking on the sidewalk. Cars zooming past his window. Green leaves on the trees. Freshly mowed grass. He exited the bus when it stopped and went into the bank.

The lobby was beautiful. Brass frames around the teller windows. Brass banisters holding the red satin ropes. A black and white tile floor shining in the overhead light. Glowing stained glass windows. An old-fashioned art deco feeling.

Jackson waited in line. When it was his turn, he stepped up to the window.

"How can I help you?" the young woman on the other side asked.

"I need to rent a safe deposit box."

"How big and for how long?"

"What's the smallest size and how much?" Jackson asked.

"Right now, six inches by ten inches and a foot long." The teller tapped her pencil on the counter. "There's a special rate if you sign an extended contract."

"How much?"

"For five years, fifty cents a month. That's half the normal rate."

Jackson thought for a second. He had no idea where he would be in five years. "How much for fifty years?" *That will give me plenty of time.*

The woman looked askance at him. "Fifty?"

"Yes. In cash."

"Give me a few minutes to find out." The woman left the window.

Jackson leaned against the counter and watched the people. He didn't want to be caught unaware if something happened. This was a bank and they did get robbed.

"Sir?" said a female voice.

"Huh?" Jackson turned around. "Yes, ma'am."

The woman pushed a form across the counter. "Sign here. A fifty-year rental is two hundred dollars."

"Thanks." Jackson signed his name, wrote Mangus Malone as another person with access and returned the form.

The woman pushed two keys across the counter. "Here. The box is 622."

"How do I put stuff in? And when?"

"You can access your box only during working hours. It's a two-party system. You have the keys. Go to the teller window. Tell him or her you want to access your safe deposit box. The manager will take you into the vault."

Jackson stuck the keys in his pocket. He would come back tomorrow with Mangus so he would know too. No way would he carry his parents' special belongings on a bus. They were irreplaceable.

Two hours later

Jackson opened the front door to Mangus' quarters. A two-bedroom house in officer country at Camp Pendleton. The house was quiet. *Uncle Manny must still be at the office.* He shut the door and went to his room. It contained a twin bed, an area rug, and a dresser. Nothing else. Just white walls and wood floors.

Hungry after the long day, Jackson went to the kitchen and made a peanut butter sandwich. His godfather didn't keep much in the pantry.

Only a few staples. He ate at the mess hall for breakfast and lunch then the officer's club for dinner. Cooking was not in his wheelhouse.

Munching on the sandwich, he went into the living room. It was sparse as well. A radio, fabric couch, end table, and one overstuffed leather chair with a hassock. Jackson turned on the radio and picked up the latest copy of *Leatherneck Magazine* from the stack on the end table next to the couch. He sat down to read.

The sun got lower and lower through the open window blinds. Jackson switched on the floor lamp beside him to add light to the darkening room.

A few minutes later, the front door opened. Mangus came into the living room in his Service A green uniform. "Hey, kid. Did you get everything done?"

"Yeah, sold the car and got the safe deposit box. I listed you as a signer so you can get into it if needed. Can you take me tomorrow to put Mom and Dad's stuff in it?" Jackson handed him a key.

Mangus stuck the key in his pocket. "Sure…hang on. I have something for you." He disappeared into his bedroom.

Jackson went back to his magazine. He looked up when Mangus stopped in front of him.

"These are yours. Jim insisted I give them to you." Mangus placed two tri-folded flags in Jackson's lap. "The top one is your dad's and the bottom one is your mom's."

Unable to find his voice, Jackson gripped the flags to his chest. He wanted so badly to be at the funeral with Jim. To touch the caskets. To throw in a handful of dirt. To lay his mother's favorite flower, a red rose on her casket. To place his Distinguished Honor Graduate certificates in his dad's hand to be with him forever. Above all, he wanted to say goodbye. To say he loved them in person. To have some sort of closure. Yet another thing taken away from him by that damn war.

Mangus sat on the couch beside him and put an arm across his shoulders. "Just let it out, son. It's just us this time. No one to intrude or tell you to suck it up. Your dad gave me this bit of advice at my father's funeral. Grief is not a sign of weakness. It's the price of love. You loved James and Kim with your entire being, and it will always hurt, but you'll never be alone. I promise."

Jackson sniffed. He was a combat-hardened soldier. He'd seen the nine circles of hell in one year. He tried to hold back the tears. To be a man. He couldn't. The dam burst, and he leaned into Mangus' shoulder and cried. It was the only way for him to move forward with his life. To get rid of the grief. He couldn't purge the loneliness of his heart. That would only come with time.

CHAPTER 11

July 7, 1953
West Point, NY – United States Military Academy
Reception Day

Jackson glanced around as Uncle Manny drove his 1950 green Chevy Bel-Air past the Thayer Hotel. Once on the West Point grounds, the scenery changed from one of civilian normalcy to that of meticulously manicured lawns, monuments, and military precision. He was minutes away from setting his dream into motion.

Mangus pulled up in front of an arrowed sign labeled *Candidates Report Here* with men lined up next to it. "We're here."

"I can see that. Thanks, Uncle Manny. It was nice to spend a week with you outside of Pendleton."

"Same here, kid." Mangus shook Jackson's hand. "Write Sara as much as possible so she doesn't worry about you and call when you can. Collect."

"Yes, sir." Jackson climbed out of the car and pulled his green duffle bag out of the back seat. He put on his garrison cap, straightened his Ike jacket, and slung the bag over his shoulder. It contained everything he owned. All of it Army issue, except for one set of civilian clothing. Jeans, cowboy boots, sneakers, and a button-up denim shirt.

His parents' flags he left with Uncle Manny to take back to the Double M. He bought flag cases with the last of his money. They needed to be displayed. To be seen. So his parents would never be forgotten.

Jackson stepped back and saluted his godfather.

Mangus nodded in return, waved, then put the car into gear and left the way he came. As promised, he didn't go in.

A cadet in a gray jacket and white trousers with a red sash around his waist approached him. "See a lot of action in Korea? You have a DSC, Silver Star, Soldier's Medal, two Purple Hearts, Jump wings, Infantry cord, and a Combat Infantry Badge." He pointed at Jackson's right sleeve. "And two overseas service bars."

"Yeah, just got home a few weeks ago."

"Are you one of the new Sergeants assigned to the Point? You don't have to be in this line. It's for the FNGs."

"FNGs?" He knew that meant fucking new guys.

"Yeah, fourth years, plebes, new meat."

Jackson smiled. "Then I'm an FNG, fourth year, plebe, new meat."

The cadet looked him up and down. "Really? You're too squared away."

"Yes, really." Jackson held up his packet with *Transferred to West Point-Cadet* stamped on the cover.

The cadet nodded. "Then take your place in line."

"Thanks." Jackson knew he was in for it later. Didn't matter. After being in combat, he could take anything they could dish out. With the line of new cadets extending behind him, Jackson went to the end and set his duffle bag on the ground. In front of him stood another young man dressed like him. The same Army issue duffle bag was sitting on the ground beside him. He tapped the corporal on the shoulder.

The corporal turned and acknowledged him with a nod.

Jackson held out his hand. "Sergeant Jackson MacKenzie, late of the 1st Cavalry Division."

The young man smiled and shook his hand. "Corporal Chris Patterson, 82nd Airborne. Nice to meet you."

"Did you just come back from Korea like me?"

"No. Served with the 3rd Infantry Division. Got back in January, went to Airborne School then transferred to the 82nd."

Jackson leaned to one side then the other. Patterson had the blue and white diagonal-striped patch of the 3rd on his right shoulder like he had the 25th Infantry Division on his. Since he saw combat with the 25th, he was entitled to wear the patch. The 1st Cavalry Division patch he wore proudly on his left shoulder as his current, no, former unit. Today, he became a West Point cadet.

Patterson tapped Jackson's ribbons with an awe-struck look on his face. "DSC, Silver Star, Soldier's Medal, and two Purple Hearts. You impressed the hell out of someone."

"Yeah." Jackson chuckled. "A lot of someones. That's how I got here."

The line moved forward as another cadet with a clipboard checked off names. When Jackson got to him, the cadet asked, "Name," in a loud voice that boded no arguments.

"Sergeant MacKenzie, Jackson J."

The cadet looked up. "Only your parents need to know your first name. And you are no longer a sergeant. From now on, until you get past Beast Barracks, you're New Cadet MacKenzie. Got that?"

Jackson winced. "Sir, yes, sir," he yelled. *Guess he doesn't know about my parents.*

"At least you're not as much of a dumb smackhead as the others and know how to pop off." The cadet pointed at the arched opening in the granite wall a few feet away. "Go. Now!"

"Yes, sir." Jackson shouldered his duffle bag then followed Patterson through the sally port past the line of senior cadets waving them forward. At least he didn't have to worry about losing his hair. He'd already shaved it off to a recruit cut before he got here. Why give the barber a chance to nick his scalp?

It was going to be a long day but not as long as the one on Old Baldy. That day and night went on forever. And he nearly died. If he could get through that, he could get through anything the senior cadets could dish out. Yelling, pushups, sit-ups, and forced marches for punishment. Been there. Done that. Lived to tell about it with sore muscles. Now he was ready to become a member of the Long Gray Line. First, he had to survive reporting to a Cadet in the Red Sash.

"Step up to my line. Do not step on my line. Do not step over my line. Step up to my line," yelled a chiseled, muscular senior cadet, waving him forward with his hand. He said the words so fast they were almost unintelligible.

The man was built like a linebacker. Huge and imposing. Bulging shoulders and arms like a Greek god. His uniform, white trousers, and a gray wool jacket with a black stripe in the center that hung straight and tailored. On his hands, bright white gloves. His black glossy shoes reflected light like a mirror. A gray service cap with a black band and West Point cadet shield on his head. Around his waist, a red sash. The badge of his rank, his time at West Point. A Firstie. He glared at Jackson from under the black brim of his service cap placed exactly two fingers above his eyebrows.

Jackson stepped up to the white tape line on the ground. The hot sun beat on his shaved head. Sweat dripped down his neck. To keep from confusing him with the assigned enlisted personnel, they made him change out of his uniform at the quartermaster's office. His current clothing, black workout shorts, black low quarter dress shoes, black socks, and a white t-shirt, the West Point crest on the left side of his chest. He had no idea what building was in front of him. It was gray/tan granite, majestic, old gothic architecture. Beautiful. Almost glowing in the bright sunlight. Two steps above him stood the senior cadet. Knuckles white on his clenched fists.

"Drop your bag," the cadet ordered.

Jackson unslung his newly issued duffle bag filled with his new academy clothing from his back. The one containing his Army-issued stuff had been taken away during processing. The Army first sergeant in charge promised to place it in his room with his service dress uniform. He dropped the duffle bag next to his feet, making sure it didn't go over the tape line. The DMZ between him and the Firstie. The line of demarcation. Of success or failure. Of yelling or silence.

"Re...port," the cadet bellowed at near eardrum bursting levels. He leaned forward. His hot breath hit Jackson's face. It stank of cigarettes, garlic, and...milk.

Jackson saluted, as he had done so many times in the past to his superiors. Right hand to his forehead, fingers straight and together, palm canted toward his eyes, arm straight to his elbow. His left arm at his side, hand cupped. "Sir, New Cadet MacKenzie reports to the Cadet in the Red Sash for the first time as ordered."

The cadet looked at him, confused. As if he didn't expect him to get it right on the first try. He cocked his head one way then another.

Jackson maintained his salute, unmoving, waiting for his orders. After this, he could only respond in four ways to a senior cadet, Yes, sir – No, sir – No excuse, sir – Sir, I do not understand. Along with everything from the New Cadet knowledge book, *Bugle Notes*. Ranks, he fully understood, same with Army units and patches. And he knew the makeup of units by heart. He lived it. Four squads made a platoon, four platoons made a company. Three companies made up a battalion, three battalions made a regiment, and three regiments make up a division. Why did he need to know there were 340 lights in Cullum Hall or there were 92.2 million gallons of water flowing from the spillway into Lusk Reservoir? The answer to the *how is the cow* question made him want to laugh. *Sir, she walks, she talks, she's full of chalk, the lacteal fluid extracted from the female of the bovine species is highly prolific to the nth degree.* Thank goodness for his photographic memory.

"Move out, New Cadet. I haven't got all day," the senior cadet yelled.

Jackson picked up his duffle bag, put it on his back, and turned. Behind him, the other new cadets, waiting for their turn with a Cadet with the Red Sash. Sheep with wide eyes, dark pupils, ready for the slow and painful slaughter. He headed for the barracks, ran up five flights of stairs, and went into the room indicated on his paperwork.

The room smelled of strong bleach. The white linoleum floor, dull and yellow from the multi-coatings of wax. On one wall, a dresser with drawers. A gray metal desk was jammed into the corner of one wall next to a worn, stained twin mattress on a metal frame, then another desk, and a twin bunk. Stacked on each bunk, folded bed linen, towels stenciled in black with a name, and a green laundry bag.

Hmm... Jackson set his duffle bag on the bunk next to the window. His name was on the towels. His old Army duffle bag, his rank and last name stenciled in black on the side, sat in the corner. His Ike jacket with ribbons, matching pants, khaki shirt, and tie hung in the open coat closet. *At least they kept the promise. Probably because of my war record.* He looked out the window. The parade ground stretched green into a field of trees. An American flag fluttered in the wind between Storm King Mountain and Breakneck Ridge. The Hudson River stood out on the other side. A half-mile-wide strip of muddy-looking water with a steep bluff you didn't want to get near if you wanted to live. You'd make a big, bloody splat at the bottom of the cliff.

Another cadet came in and shut the door, dressed in the same clothing as him. Corporal Patterson. He looked at Jackson with a slight smile then set his duffle bag on his bunk. "Interesting first day."

"Yeah. Have any problems with the cadet in the red sash?"

"Nope. You?"

"No. He looked flustered when I did it right."

"Same here. Guess we don't have another roommate."

"Noticed that," Jackson replied.

Two sharp, rapid-fire knocks sounded on the doorframe.

"Room, attention," Jackson yelled as he snapped to attention with Patterson. "Enter, sir."

The door opened and a cadet in the same uniform as earlier with the red sash around his waist entered the room. From the rank on both shoulders, a single chevron, he was a sergeant.

The cadet nodded. "At ease." He removed his gray service hat and set it on the dresser. "You two know the drill and are ahead of the other plebes by a mile. I'm your squad leader for New Cadet Barracks, Cadet Mullins."

"Yes, sir," Jackson and Patterson replied.

"Behind closed doors, like now, I won't be as strict. I'll treat you like a cadet, not a plebe. More of an equal. I may pick your brains about the battles you've participated in. The tactics used. Especially you, MacKenzie. Your status as war veterans is why your tactical officer put you two together. You've been in the trenches. Seen death. In front of the other plebes, you get treated like everyone else. Got it?"

"Yes, sir," they said together.

"Like in the answer to the question, what do plebes rank?" Jackson said.

"Yes…which is what, New Cadet MacKenzie?"

"Sir, the Superintendent's dog, the Commandant's cat, the waiters in the Mess Hall, the Hell Cats, the Generals in the Air Force, and all the Admirals in the whole damned Navy."

Mullins smiled. "Excellent, you've been studying your knowledge book."

"Yes, sir. Permission to ask a question," Jackson asked.

"Go ahead, MacKenzie."

"Why isn't there a third bunk in here? I was told there were three to a room."

"Same reason as before. Both of you earned it by serving in Korea with distinction and honor. Anything else?" Mullins grabbed his service hat.

"No, sir."

"MacKenzie, after the march to the Battle Monument at Trophy Point for the oath, once you're dismissed, report to the administration building."

"For what, sir?" *That's strange.*

"To see the psychologist for an IQ test at the request of the superintendent. Seems you made quite the impression on your CO in the 1st Cav, General Walker. Understood?"

"Yes, sir." *That's why the general asked that question. Better take my A-game*

"Now with the pleasantries over, get into your black shirts, tie, and gray pants. I don't need to tell you how to wear the uniform, right?"

"No, sir," Jackson and Patterson replied. That was old hat to someone after a year in the Army.

"Don't forget to put your nameplates on your shirts." Mullins looked at his watch. "I have two hours to get the rest of your knucklehead classmates in some semblance of a squad formation and teach them to march like soldiers. Don't be surprised if I use one or both of you as an example of how to march at 120 beats a minute, turn, salute, cover, and stand at attention. Understood?"

"Yes, sir," they replied together.

"Good. Just a tidbit of information. Since you two are tall, you're assigned to the 1st New Cadet Company, which is a flanker company. You have five minutes to get dressed and outside your room with your backs against the wall standing at attention. The others have three, so get moving and show your classmates what being a soldier really looks like."

Jackson and Patterson snapped to attention. "Yes, sir."

They opened their duffle bags and pulled out their black shirts, gray pants, white t-shirts, and gray service caps. Dressed in less than two minutes, they were out in the hall before the rest of the cadets even opened their doors. Seconds ticked by. Jackson glanced at Patterson as a symphony of clunks, bangs, crashes, and curses came from the other rooms.

Mullins walked by them with a small smile. He continued down the hall. "Get your slimy asses out here before I kick them all the way to the ocean," he yelled.

Jackson winked at Patterson. "Guess basic training was good for something besides getting yelled at," he whispered.

"Yeah," Patterson replied.

They squared their shoulders, straightened their backs, and stood like statues as their uncoordinated classmates ran into the hall looking like soup sandwiches. All thumbs. Knocking each other down in their haste to stand at attention against the wall.

Jackson maintained his stone face but smiled inwardly. *Things are about to get interesting. Let the yelling and hazing begin.*

CHAPTER 12

August 29, 1953
West Point – United States Military Academy Stable

Jackson stood at attention outside of the stable. While waiting for Coach Benson, he thought about his score on the IQ test, 172. The psychologist said it was in the genius level range, on par with Albert Einstein. His was estimated between 160-190. A winner of the Nobel Prize. The man who developed the theories of special and general relativity. The theory of relativity. $E=mc^2$. One of the two pillars of modern physics. He didn't feel that smart. Just a normal, fallible guy. And according to the upperclassmen, a smack, dumbsmack, smackhead, beaner, beanhead, meathead, and any other name that came to mind.

The psychologist, an expatriate from Great Britain, said he was sending the test results to MENSA, whatever that meant.

Yesterday was acceptance day. A-day, and the presentation parade or in academy parlance, p-rade. The day his class finished Beast Barracks and accepted by the upperclassmen into the Corps of Cadets as Plebes, fourth-class cadets. He wouldn't miss the days on end with upperclassmen screaming in his face. A mentally draining experience when everything covered was the same things he learned in basic training and a year in Korea as a squad leader. The 100th night seemed so far away right now.

He made a mental list of things he hated during those seven grueling weeks. Saturday room inspection, a SAMI. His TAC officer, Captain Hickey, always found dust in the most unlikely places, crevices even a tiny spider wouldn't fit through. Evening shower formations lined against the walls in their robes with a towel draped over their right arms and chins tucked in. "Grabbing some wrinkles," they called it. Endless hours of practice hikes through the hills made him feel like he was back at Fort Benning being harassed by the drill sergeants. Every muscle rebelled against him, aching to the bone when he went to bed.

One thing he didn't need was time on the bayonet course at Morgan's Farm. He'd stuck bayonets and his trench knife into real men, not ones made of straw, then watched them die with their guts hanging out. That brought back bad memories of the war. Ones that he wanted to forget.

He knew from experience the high-intensity physical training was meant to challenge his classmates. To build their foundation as one lays a

97

brick wall for the years to come. It was less of a physical challenge for him than a mental one. Dealing with young men his age who knew nothing about being a leader tried his patience. The combat-hardened coldness from the battlefield. They knew nothing about military standards and courtesies. Things ingrained into him from a young age.

To many of his classmates, the code of ethics were words written on a piece of paper. Something to sign. Not something they would live by at the academy and for the rest of their lives. Those new cadets learned fast that ethics were more than hokey words. The Firsties made sure they understood it was a strict code. Unbreakable. He already knew that code. His father taught him through his very actions. Duty before all else, except honor. Duty, Honor, Country. The motto of West Point.

Last week, every company of new cadets marched out on Jefferson Road through the Washington Gate in fatigues and a helmet with an M1 slung over their shoulder. The Plebe hike. It was such a relief to have five days in the field away from West Point's gray walls. This was the final trial of Beast Barracks. Camping out like soldiers, living in tents around lakes and smelly cow pastures in New York and Connecticut. The odor of cattle actually helped him to relax. It felt more like the good times at the Double M Ranch.

A man in a black and gold West Point warm-up jacket walked up and stopped in front of him. "You must be Cadet MacKenzie."

"Sir, yes, sir," Jackson replied, maintaining his position of attention.

"At ease, MacKenzie."

"Yes, sir." Jackson put his hands behind his back.

"I read your record with the American Horse Shows Association. Quite impressive. You started on a Welsh pony and moved on to a Quarter horse. Eighteen wins, twelve seconds, seven thirds, and numerous top tens. Shows me you're an excellent rider. Any other riding experience?"

"Yes, sir. Western, roping, reining, and driving cattle on my godfather's ranch in Montana."

Coach Benson laughed. "So there's a bit of a cowboy in you."

"Yes, sir." Jackson let out a hint of a smile. He was.

"Okay, here's the plan. Boyer has saddled his horse, Bingo. Change into the used riding pants and boots in the barn. Use the helmet. If I like what I see and select you for the team, we'll get you new gear. Understood?"

"Yes, sir."

"One more thing, you'll have to follow the New Cadet Program to the letter before even thinking about being an important member of one of our athletic squads."

"Yes, sir."

Coach Benson pointed at the barn door. "Go. I don't have all day."

Jackson went into the barn to change. He had a chance. A slim one as a plebe. Now he had to make the most of it with his riding skills.

Cadet Boyer handed Jackson the reins to Bingo, a sixteen-hand, dark bay warmblood Hanoverian stallion. He put his left foot in the stirrup and mounted the horse. For a few seconds, he sat there. Gauging the horse and his reaction to him as a rider. The horse remained still and unfazed.

Jackson clicked his tongue and guided the horse around the pasture. Bingo was light on his feet and responsive to his heels, hands, and leg pressure. He eased the horse into a gallop. Bingo was also fast. His gallop seemed to float with nary a bounce.

At the other end of the pasture, he pulled Bingo to a stop. Slowly, he rode back to where Coach Benson and Cadet Boyer were standing.

Jackson guided the horse in a large circle. He reversed course and went in the opposite direction. *Let's see what this horse can do.* He queued Bingo into a piaffe.

Bingo trotted in place, moving neither forward nor backward.

Nice. He started the horse forward again and queued him into a half-pass at a canter. They moved forward and sideways at the same time.

I need to make an impression. Jackson threw in a flying leg change. With all four feet in the air, Bingo skipped, changing his right lead leg to his left.

Feeling the need to show off, Jackson changed direction then did a pirouette and a passage. Bingo's legs exploded from the ground as he moved across the ground at a highly elevated and extremely powerful trot.

He stopped Bingo and rode back to Coach Benson.

Benson's expression remained impartial for a few seconds. That worried him. Then a large smile spread across Benson's face. Boyer's too.

"Very nice. It's rare to see someone do that with a horse they've never ridden before. You have a natural ability with horses and it shows in your smooth riding," Benson said.

"Yes, sir." Jackson tried to keep himself from smiling but couldn't. He felt so at ease on the back of a horse. It was relaxing. As if he were meant to be there.

"I've set up some jumps in the corner of the pasture. Just go left to right over them. I want to see your technique."

"Yes, sir." Jackson rode to the jumps and circled them once to take a look. There were only four. All three feet high. Beginner jumps. Easy for this horse.

He sent the horse into a gallop. His smooth gait and rhythm sent him over the first jump by a good two feet. The second, third, and fourth jump went just as easily.

Jackson galloped out, rode back to Coach Benson, and stopped. He dismounted Bingo and handed the reins to Boyer. "Want me to cool him out for you."

"I'll take care of it. Coach wants to talk to you." Boyer led Bingo into the stable.

"Walk with me, MacKenzie," Benson said.

"Yes, sir." Jackson slowed his pace beside the shorter man.

"You're really talented, son. You sit a horse like you're a part of it."

"Thank you, sir."

"I'll forward my decision to the Tactical Department." Benson stopped and held out his hand. "Welcome to the team."

Jackson shook Benson's hand. "Yes, sir. Thank you, sir."

"Come back tomorrow at 0800 after breakfast. You'll meet your horse and the rest of the team then. This will cover your athletic requirement unless you plan on trying out for something else."

"I was thinking about the track team. I was a pretty good middle-distance runner in high school. Set the school record for the 880-yard run and the mile. Will I have that kind of time?"

"Not really, since this includes taking care of the horses. If you want to train during what free time you have, it'll be a good way for you to stay in shape. The endurance and weight room work will help with your riding."

"Training is fine, sir. I'd much rather do this."

Benson smiled. "So would I. You might be good at running but you excel at riding."

"Thank you, sir."

"Wear your sweats tomorrow. Plan on getting dirty. Dismissed."

"Yes, sir." Jackson went back into the barn to change into his cadet uniform.

A chestnut horse with a white blaze stuck his head over a stall door at the end of the barn and neighed. He looked in Jackson's direction, his big brown eyes stared at him. Telling him, *pick me.*

Jackson went to him and looked at the name on the stall door. Firefly. The horse was big. Well over sixteen hands and pushing fourteen hundred pounds. Powerfully built with rippling muscles. White socks nearly to his knees on all four legs. He petted the horse's neck. "Wish I had some peppermints for you, boy. You're beautiful."

Firefly snorted.

"You agree, huh? See you tomorrow." *I'll snag a few sugar cubes from the mess hall in the morning.* "Hope you're mine. We'll do great things together. I can already tell."

August 30, 1953
West Point – United States Military Academy Stable

Jackson entered the stable and joined the loose formation of cadets standing near the office. They were all whispering to each other. He didn't know anyone except Boyer, so he stayed silent, off to one side.

Coach Benson came out of the office. "Welcome back, everyone. First, I want to introduce our new team member, Cadet Jackson MacKenzie."

Jackson raised his hand. "Hi, everyone."

"Before any of you say anything…yes, Cadet MacKenzie is a plebe. But he came to us via Korea as a sergeant in the 1st Calvary Division. Highly decorated for valor with the DSC, Silver Star, Soldier's Medal, and two Purple Hearts. He's been in the thick of it, so treat him with the respect due. MacKenzie is also the best rider I've seen come down the pike in years. He's won some highly prestigious meets in the under sixteen ranks of the American Horse Shows Association."

Cadet Boyer raised his hand. "What horse is he getting?"

Coach Benson pointed at the big chestnut stallion Jackson petted yesterday. "Firefly."

The other cadets broke out in rambunctious laughter.

Jackson tapped Boyer's shoulder. "What's so funny?"

Boyer swallowed. "No one rides Firefly. He refuses to jump and won't learn dressage patterns."

"Really? I looked at him yesterday. Seems smart."

Benson joined them. "That's the problem. He's too smart. Firefly is fast and powerful but flopped on the track as a racehorse. He refused to go into the starting gate and dumped his jockey more than once then raced down the track on his own. The outriders had to catch him. His owner graduated from the Point and donated him to us. All he's done since he got here two years ago is eat and shit."

Jackson raised an eyebrow. "And you're giving him to me?"

"Yes, I think he's waiting for that special rider. That bond. A connection. Two souls meeting as one. I saw him greet you yesterday. He's never done that before. So I think he's already picked you."

"I'll take him."

"Once we get done mucking the stalls and feeding and brushing the horses, I want you to saddle Firefly and see what he does. See if I'm reading him right."

Jackson grinned. "Can't wait, coach."

"Everyone, go take care of your mounts. Boyer, show MacKenzie where everything is and get him a saddle and tack. Then take care of Bingo."

Boyer nodded. "Got it, coach." He waved Jackson forward. "Follow me."

Jackson saddled Firefly and led him to the same pasture as yesterday. The jumps were still set up on the other end. The cadets and Coach Benson were lined up next to the fence.

He mounted Firefly and sat with a loose rein, waiting to see what the horse would do. If he would spook, try to run, buck him off, or turn his head and try to bite him.

Firefly stood still, only swishing his tail.

Jackson snugged up on the reins and urged the horse forward with a click of his tongue, leg pressure, and heels.

Firefly took off at a walk. If Jackson thought Bingo's gait was smooth, riding Firefly was like gliding on air. No bounce. Feet like feathers going over the ground. Hooves barely touching before the leg came up. Fleet-footed and nimble, he turned on a dime.

"Let's see what you can do, boy." Jackson urged him into a gallop.

Fast didn't describe Firefly's speed. Greased lightning did. Supersonic. It took Jackson's breath away. He guided Firefly over to the jumps. With almost no effort at all, the horse went over all four, at speed, no hint of refusal. Clearing the top rail by over three feet.

Jackson pulled Firefly up. He wanted to see if the horse could do any dressage moves at all. "Show me what you can do, boy." He queued Firefly into a piaffe.

Firefly trotted in place, moving neither forward nor backward. Smooth and nary a jar.

"So you have been paying attention. I knew you were smart." He urged the horse forward and queued him into a half-pass at a canter. They went forward and sideways at the same time. Firefly did the move even better than Bingo.

Jackson wanted to try something. He queued a flying leg change. With all four feet in the air, Firefly skipped, changing his left lead leg to his right.

Now to see if they taught Firefly everything. Jackson eased him in a pirouette then a passage. Firefly's legs lifted off the ground as if shot from a gun. His trot was so elevated his knees nearly touched his chest. Powerful and strong, they moved across the ground as if turbo-charged.

Jackson pulled him up in the center of the field. *I got the best horse in the barn.* He rode back to the coach and dismounted. Firefly placed his head on Jackson's shoulder. Eyeing the other cadets, almost protective. Guarding.

Coach Benson smiled. "Just like I thought. He chose you. Water him down, take him in, and cool him out. I'll get your riding gear and a new saddle ordered. Use that one until they come in. Great job out there, MacKenzie."

Jackson nodded. "Thank you, coach." He fed the horse a sugar cube and led him into the barn. This made the last seven weeks worth it. They would have fun together over the next four years.

September 10, 1953
West Point Cadet Barracks

Jackson checked his schedule tacked to the corkboard above his desk. It was going to be a long day. A long week. And a long four years.

Week 1 (Alternate week 1 and 2 classes)
0400 Get up, make the bed, clean the room, read the newspaper for formation questions
0430 Report to stable, clean stalls, feed, and groom horses
0530 Shower, dress
0605 Report to formation

0615 Breakfast
0755 - 0915 Mathematics Mon-Sat
0955 - 1155 Military Topography and Graphics Tues/Thur
0930 - 1015 Physical Education, Mon/Wed/Fri/Sat
1200 - Lunch formation
1205 - Lunch
1300 - 1400 English Mon/Wed/Fri
1300 - 1400 Foreign Language - Russian Tues/Thur
1415 - 1515 Tactics Mon/Fri
1430 - 1730 Stable. Practice dressage patterns, Tues/Wed/Thur
1530 - 1730 Stable. Practice jumping, Mon/Fri
1750 - Report for dinner formation
1805 - Dinner
1900 - Call to quarters (Study and homework time)
2300 - Taps
0000 - Lights Out

Week 2
0755 - 0915 Mathematics Mon-Sat
0955 - 1155 Military Topography and Graphics Mon/Wed/Fri
0930 - 1015 Physical Education Tues/Thur/Sat
1300 - 1400 Foreign Language Mon/Wed/Fri
1300 - 1400 English Tues/Thur
1415 - 1515 Tactics Tues/Thur
1430 - 1730 Stable - practice dressage patterns, Mon/Wed/Fri
1530 - 1730 Stable - practice jumping, Tues/Thur
1300 – 1600 (non-game Saturday) Stable - practice dressage patterns/jumping
0930 – 1130 (Game weekend, Sunday) Stable - practice dressage patterns/jumping

Study time till 1515 when not in class
After 1515 - Cadet free time

At breakfast inside Washington Hall, Jackson stood next to his ten-person table to the right of the Cold Beverage Corporal, waiting for the command to take seats.

In the center of the dining hall stood the poop-deck. A granite structure that reminded him of the rampart of a medieval castle. The place from where all announcements were read to the Corps.

Fifty feet above his head hung enormous chandeliers. The large arched windows let in natural light. Forty-eight state flags were suspended from poles attached to the walls. Battle flags carried by United States Army units adorned special places in the hall. Each one marred by bullet holes, cuts, and scorch marks.

Covering the entire back wall of the southwest wing was a mural depicting the twenty most decisive battles in world history. In the north wing was a stained glass window titled, *The Life of George Washington*. A WPA project completed in 1937. Portraits of the former West Point superintendents held places of prominence and reflection.

"Take seats!"

Jackson sat on the last three inches of his chair with his eyes fixed on the academy crest at the top of his plate. Any deviation would invite the wrath of an upperclassman. He performed his table duties as the Coffee or Warm Beverage Corporal, pouring coffee into the upperclassmen's mugs and keeping the pot full. Part of his job included evenly distributing all items at each end of the table. Another duty, warming the toast by placing it under the coffee pot and mashing it down to melt the butter.

The plebe at the foot of the table, the Gunner, Cadet Mailer, received a plate of scrambled eggs from the waiter. "Sir, the scrambled eggs are on the table, scrambled eggs for the head of the table, sir," he announced then passed the platter to the table commandant, Cadet Captain Elwood.

Elwood served himself, passed the plate to his left, then it zig-zagged around the table, going among the classes from first to fourth.

Cadet Corporal Casey Hoskins, a second-classman, aka cow, and in Jackson's flanker company, A-1, approached him. He was tall and skinny with a face full of pimples. Slowly, he leaned into Jackson's face. His hot breath stank of cheap cigarettes with a hint of whiskey. Alcohol was forbidden in the cadet area. So much for the regulations. "Tell me what article you read in the New York Times this morning."

Jackson squared his shoulders. "Sir, it was reported in the New York Times the fifth Soviet atomic bomb test was detected by the US on August 23rd."

"What are the three general orders?"

Jackson sucked in a deep breath. "Sir. One, I will guard everything within the limits of my post and quit my post only when properly relieved. Two, I will obey my special orders and perform all of my duties in a military manner. Three, I will report violations of my special orders, emergencies, and anything not covered in my instructions to the commander of the relief."

Hoskins cocked his head. "Give me your quill. It's time for a write-up, mackerel snapper." Each word bit off and monotone.

Huh? "Sir? I gave you the correct answer."

"Did I speak to you, Cadet MacKenzie?"

Jackson's neck felt as if it was on fire. "No, sir." He handed over a square piece of paper he was required to keep folded neatly in his pocket notebook. This was his first entry. And, hopefully, his last.

Hoskins scribbled on one page and handed it back. He returned to his chair and sat down.

As the meal continued, Jackson performed his duties. He didn't falter, even when the seven upper-class cadets did a switch-up, changing from coffee to hot chocolate. After returning to his seat, he ate at attention, squaring off his arm movements, taking baby bites, and chewing the requisite three times before swallowing. All the while, listening to the conversations of the other cadets. He needed to know what was being said.

His name came up in hushed words between Hoskins and Elwood. Something about him making a mistake when asked the three general orders. He made no mistake. Every recruit at basic training learned those verbatim. Repeating them back to the drill instructors at the top of their lungs. Time and time again.

Elwood got up after finishing his meal. He marched to where Jackson sat at the end of the table. "Cadet MacKenzie."

Jackson stood so fast his chair tipped over on the slick floor, sending him toppling over with it. He picked himself up off the floor but didn't brush himself off, not with the captain eyeballing him like a pig on a spit, and stood at attention. His ears were ringing, and his neck hurt from the hard knock against the floor, sending pain through his upper back and shoulders like a hot knife through butter. "Yes, sir." Although Elwood's position was meant to make him cower in fear, he would not be intimidated. Not after everything he had seen in Korea.

"With your experience, you should do a better job as a fourth-class cadet. I know you have a heavy load but…" Elwood paused to make sure everyone was listening. "That's no excuse to become a lazy smackhead. I wouldn't have believed you'd be a damn ghost. You get one more chance to prove you can be part of the Long Gray Line. Concentrate and perform like you're supposed to."

A Firstie, Lieutenant Markowitz sitting in the chair next to Jackson, put a hand on Elwood's arm. "Hey, take it easy. Give MacKenzie a break. He got the general orders correct."

Elwood jerked his arm away. "Stay out of this. This guy is a tool and it's going to stop…now."

What the hell? Jackson felt as low as dirt. He was reeling from the dressing down. Even though he had done everything right, all the energy went out of him. He felt empty. His entire being had been sucked out. He wanted to throw up. His legs went weak, his feet slid around under him on the slick floor. Then he realized what was happening. His anger rose and his blood boiled. He felt lightheaded and drew slower breaths to keep from hyperventilating. What gave this guy the right to humiliate him? It wasn't professional or a good command style. Combat taught him how to lead men. This sure wasn't how you motivated someone under you. Unless you wanted a midnight fragging. Or a beat down in a blanket party.

"Did you hear me, MacKenzie?" Elwood yelled. The saliva in the corners of his mouth flew out.

"Yes, sir," Jackson replied. This was hazing, pure and simple. Today, he was the target. He had done his duties exactly as taught by the upperclassmen. Made it to class on time. Finished his homework. Cleaned his room and delivered the newspapers and mail. Did every maneuver in close order drill and formation, all within the West Point standards. He would withstand the psychological warfare of the upperclassmen's game and remain motivated, no matter what tricks they had up their sleeves. He didn't need that negativity as motivation. Not after Korea. And certainly not from that pencil neck Hoskins. All he could do, suck it up and play the game.

Hoskins took Elwood's place. "MacKenzie, care to try again to show us you're worthy of being a plebe?"

"Sir, yes, sir." Jackson faced Elwood. His neck hurt like the dickens, shooting pain down his back, arms, and legs.

"Okay." Hoskins pulled a set of plastic-coated flashcards from his pocket. He flipped through it then showed a card to him. "What's this?"

Jackson almost smiled at the picture. A blue and red ribbon holding a bronze cross with an eagle in the center with a scroll that read, *For Valor.* "Distinguished Service Cross, sir. I have one." *Let's see what he does now.*

Hoskins snorted and flipped out another card. This one was a purple ribbon with a gold and purple heart.

"Purple Heart, sir. I have two of those." *He doesn't know anything about me.*

"Stop being so smug." Hoskins chewed his lip. He changed to a different set of cards and held out one. A red patch, shaped like a taro leaf with a gold border and a gold lightning bolt. "What unit is that?"

Is that all he can do? Jackson almost laughed. "The 25th Infantry Division. Tropic Lightning. I served with them in Korea."

"What's this unit?" Hoskins held out a card with a black horse's head and black bar over a field of gold.

Jackson couldn't hold back his laughter. He wanted to grab those cards and throw them in Hoskins' face. That action would only get him more grief, more demerits, and possibly kicked out. So he kept his hands at his side.

"MacKenzie!" Hoskins screamed. "Can you tell me or not?"

"Sir, it's the 1st Cavalry Division. The First Team. Served with them in Korea, too, sir." *Is he making it this easy or just luck of the draw?*

Hoskins banged his fist on the table. "You passed...for now. I'll be watching you, MacKenzie. Sit."

"Yes, sir." Jackson picked up his chair and sat at attention. Since he was finished eating, he drank water.

"Look at me, MacKenzie," Hoskins said in a mockingly soft tone.

Jackson looked up as ordered. "Yes, sir."

"Remember this." Hoskins leaned into Jackson's face." I'll ask you whatever I want, whenever I want. You'd better answer with one of your four required responses. Got it?"

"Yes, sir." Jackson smiled inwardly. Hoskins seemed confused. Almost flabbergasted. A small battle won for all fourth-class plebes. At least for today. Maybe now they would leave him alone. He stood, grabbed his notebook, and headed to class.

Jackson lined up against the wall outside his room in his academy bathrobe and only his bathrobe. It was time for the plebes to make the trek to the showers in the basement. His friend, Chris Patterson, glanced to the side then back straight forward.

Hoskins walked down the line, checking to make sure they had all their required bathing items. He stopped in front of Jackson. "Did I see a smirk on your face, MacKenzie?"

"No, sir," Jackson popped off at the top of his voice. He knew better than to do anything but keep a straight face. This was the same game the drill instructors used on the recruits at basic training. The old *break you down to build you back up into a soldier* routine. He could play it with Hoskins all day long. This guy was an amateur compared to First Sergeant Bailey who used his six-foot-five height to make sure you understood.

Towering over the recruits, his deep gruff voice got the point across while looking down at them. His intense glare through narrowed eyes could make even a superhero blink.

"Remember, MacKenzie, I'm watching you."

Jackson didn't reply. He kept his chin tucked into his neck in a vertical plane until it hurt and his chest stuck out. "Bracing," they called it. He didn't want demerits for being disrespectful. But punitive neck-retraction was just plain stupid.

"Get it back farther, MacKenzie," Hoskins yelled in Jackson's face.

He couldn't dig his chin any farther into his neck without a tracheostomy. Holding his temper at bay, when the command was given, he followed his classmates to the stairwell. Their flip-flops slapped the concrete as they went down four flights of stairs. It sounded solemn and empty without the background noise of mixed conversations. No laughter or chit-chat of 18-19-year-old young men about sports or girls.

Hoskins pointed at the shower stalls. "You meatheads know the drill. Get moving."

Jackson and his fellow plebes piled into the showers. Quickly he soaped up, shaved, and rinsed. He exited, toweled off, and wrapped his thin robe around his body. Since he and his classmates were still damp, water dripping from their shorn heads, the cloth stuck to their skin. Every muscle was outlined in the thin robe, including their balls and penis. It was humiliating as Hoskins went down the line, grading them aloud like a side of beef.

"Buzzard, seen bigger on my mom's wiener dog. Tyler, nothing special. Patterson, you're average. MacKenzie...at least you excel in something other than being a tool."

Heat rose up Jackson's face to the top of his head. In basic training, the drill instructors never embarrassed them in front of others. They had some privacy in the bathroom. The only tool here was the asshole, Hoskins.

Jackson chewed on the inside of his cheek to keep quiet. He wanted to slug Hoskins. Give him an old-fashioned beat down. Not just for himself, but for his classmates. But he didn't want to get kicked out of the academy either.

As Hoskins continued down the line, a man in a summer Khaki dress uniform appeared in the doorway. Their TAC officer, Captain Hickey.

The captain walked up behind Hoskins. "Are you done yet?"

Hoskins spun around with a surprised look on his face. "Almost, sir."

Captain Hickey looked around then approached Jackson. "Is the scar on your right calf where you were wounded in Korea, MacKenzie?"

"Yes, sir," Jackson responded.

"Did it hurt?"

"Yes, sir. Not as much as this one, though." Jackson pulled his wet robe aside to reveal the dimpled scar on his chest under his left pectoral muscle.

"That from Old Baldy?"

"Yes, sir."

"Give me your honest opinion as a former NCO. Do you think this is a degrading exercise?"

Jackson gave Hoskins a sideways glance then looked at Captain Hickey. "Yes, sir."

"So do I. Hoskins, take them back to their rooms. And no more of this tonight. Understood?"

Hoskins stood like a statue in incomprehension. "Sir?"

Captain Hickey got to within two inches of Hoskins pimpled nose. "You heard me quite clearly, Hoskins. Now! And, Hoskins, I'll be watching you."

Jackson winced. That was Hoskins' favorite phrase to him. The captain must have overheard their one-sided conversation earlier.

Hoskins waved at the door. "You heard the captain. Move out."

Jackson followed Chris as the line of fourth-classmen left the room and started up the stairs. Captain Hickey pointed out the scars and asked that particular question on purpose. To show Hoskins the error of his actions. It wasn't subtle at all. More like hitting him on the head with a sledgehammer in front of a bunch of plebes. He was in for it later. Maybe not tonight since Captain Hickey was watching. But he would pay for Hoskins' screw up.

Tomorrow was another day. One that would have more hazing. Morning formation would be interesting since all plebes had to report ten minutes before the rest of the brigade. Hoskins and Elwood, the two biggest assholes of the upperclassmen, would be there to drill them on their knowledge. Again and again. One year, just one year, that's all he had to take this. Then he would be a yearling, a third-classman, and able to dish a little out. *One day, they'll get theirs.*

CHAPTER 13

November 28, 1953
Philadelphia Municipal Stadium - Army/Navy game

The day was chilly with gray overcast skies, temperatures in the 30s, and a stiff breeze. Before the game, Jackson marched in his company with the brigade in front of the 102,000 people. By the end, he was sweating under his dress gray wool trousers, jacket, service cap, and long overcoat.

Army was 6-1-1. This was the final game of the season. One more team to beat. Navy. They had won three consecutive games against Army.

As much as Jackson wanted to beat Navy, he loved his older brother so much more. Seeing him today was the most important thing in his life. He could take losing to Navy but not failing to see his brother. The only person he had left in the world. The last time he saw him, the day he boarded the train for basic training. Jim and his mother stood on the platform, waving goodbye.

The game clock moved slowly but not the Army team, playing for pride. Coach Earl Blaik and offensive coordinator Vince Lombardi had the team working like a well-oiled machine.

Jackson cheered when Navy fumbled on the first play after the kickoff. The Black Knights swarmed to the ball. Six plays later, Army struck first blood. Touchdown. He cheered even louder.

In the second quarter, Army scored again. When the gun sounded at halftime, his voice was nearly gone, hoarse and croaky like a frog.

With all the mayhem of people headed for the concessions stands, it was time for him to ditch the prying eyes of the upperclassmen. Especially Hoskins. The guy was a thorn in his ass. Even though he had received permission from his TAC officer to leave the brigade, Jackson was the lowest of the low. A plebe. Hoskins would ignore the permission slip and go after him anyway.

Jackson went under the stadium, first stopping at the bathroom to shake anyone following him. He then headed for the entrance marked 12E, the prearranged meeting place with his brother.

The crowd was thick, milling around him with drinks and snacks in their hands. Jackson looked over their heads for a familiar one. He spotted it, in a crewcut, standing off to the right of entry gate 12E. Carefully, to avoid getting anything on his uniform and gigged with pushups later, he wove his way through the mass of people. He stopped in front of his brother and came to attention. "Cadet Fourth Class MacKenzie reporting to Midshipman Second Class MacKenzie…sir!"

Jim shook his head. "Stop that, JJ. At ease."

Jackson smiled. He finally enjoyed saying, "Yes, sir," to an upperclassman.

"Come here, you little rug rat." Jim held his arms open.

Jackson enveloped him in a hug. They stood there for a long moment then stepped back.

"You've grown," Jim said huskily, ruffling what little hair he had.

"Look who's talking. You look like a bear. How tall are you now? Six-two?"

"Three. I got the height from Dad, you got the brains from Mom, little brother. And you're catching up to me again. You're every bit of six-one now and you've bulked up…a lot. Not a skinny-ass kid any longer."

"Yup." Jackson flexed his right arm.

Jim squeezed Jackson's bicep under the sleeve of his long overcoat. "Nice. Want to arm wrestle?"

"Nah. I'd rather keep my shoulder right where it is, in the socket." Jackson laughed. "You're a varsity wrestler now."

"Touché. Come on. I want my classmates to meet you. I told them all about your exploits in Korea."

"Ahh…Jim, why'd you have to do that for?"

"Because I'm proud of you, little brother." Jim waved him forward. "Come on. Do I need to make it an order, plebe?"

"No, sir!" Jackson followed his brother into the brigade of midshipmen. He stood out in Army gray in the sea of Navy blue and gold.

Jim led him to a bench and scooted past several standing second-class midshipmen.

Jackson slid past them sideways, trying not to step on their feet. It surprised him when several of those midshipmen patted him on the back.

Jim pointed at the man next to him. "This is my roommate, Carl Stanza." Then he pointed at Jackson. "Meet my little brother, Jackson."

Carl shook Jackson's hand. "Not so little anymore. I finally get to meet the hero Jim talks so much about. Welcome."

Jackson felt the heat rise in his cheeks. "Thanks." He was embarrassed that Jim bragged on him so much.

Midshipmen, both in front and behind him, introduced themselves. Jim talked about him a lot. A little nervous before surrounded by today's "enemy," Jackson felt more at ease. A member of the family. The bond of military service.

In the third quarter, Army scored again. Jackson felt awkward at that moment. He was the only one cheering. All the midshipmen around him scowled and booed. A hostile feeling fell over him and he started to leave, but Jim grabbed his arm to stop him.

"They don't mean it," Jim said.

"You sure? Feeling kind of unwanted here." Jackson looked around. "And trapped."

"Yeah. It's a rivalry, little brother, but we're all one big family."

"Uh-huh."

At the end of the game, Navy finally scored. Jackson cheered with the midshipmen. Why not? Army was going to win 20-7 and he was still in hostile territory. After the Army victory cannon fired, he followed Jim down to the field with the other midshipmen where they joined up with the Corps of Cadets. Together, both brigades sang the Navy alma mater. The tradition for the losing team. Then everyone sang Army's.

As they made their way out of the stadium, a Navy captain was standing at gate 12E. Jim stopped in front of him. Jackson stood beside his brother.

"Jackson, this is my academic advisor, Captain Hayes," Jim said.

Captain Hayes rubbed his chin. "Hmm. I like what I see. You should've joined the Navy in the Marine option program." He looked Jackson up and down then held out his hand. "It's nice to meet you, Cadet MacKenzie. Midshipman MacKenzie speaks very highly of you. I've been trading info with the West Point staff, keeping tabs on you for your brother. You're doing well, son. Keep up the good work. Remember, if you decide to change, we'll take you."

Jackson gave him a small smile as he shook the captain's hand. "Yes, sir." *Not going to happen.*

"MacKenzie!" a familiar voice screamed. Hoskins.

Jackson cringed. He wasn't the only one who turned to look behind him. Jim did too.

"Upperclassman?" Captain Hayes asked.

"Yes, sir. A third year," Jackson replied.

"Don't acknowledge him. You're speaking with me. If he can't tell a Navy captain at this distance, he needs an eye transplant. That's rude and unbecoming of a West Point cadet. He'll pay the consequences for it too."

Jackson nodded and kept his focus on Captain Hayes. This was going to be a good show.

Hoskins circled around until he was standing next to Captain Hayes. "What are you doing, MacKenzie? You're missing from your company."

Captain Hayes tapped Hoskins on the shoulder. "And what are you supposed to do in front of an officer, Cadet Hoskins, is it?"

Hoskins glanced at Captain Hayes' shoulder boards and snapped to attention. Not a sound exited his mouth it was screwed so tightly shut.

Captain Hayes walked around Hoskins. "Much better. And to answer your question, Cadet MacKenzie's been speaking with me. Do you have a problem with that?"

"No, sir," Hoskins replied.

"Good."

"By your leave, sir, but Cadet MacKenzie is a plebe."

"I know. So does his brother, Midshipman Second Class MacKenzie, the man standing beside him. You just disrespected Midshipman MacKenzie and me."

"His brother?" Hoskins glanced up at Jim and swallowed. "You're his brother?"

"Yeah." Jim clenched his fists.

Jackson wanted to laugh but didn't out of respect. Jim outweighed Hoskins by a good eighty pounds. His brother was scowling. It was quite apparent Jim wanted to use his ham-sized fist on Hoskins' head like a post-hole driver. He thought his brother might take a swing at Hoskins and placed a hand on his arm. "Jim, I'll go."

"No," Jim growled.

"I'll take care of this." Captain Hayes glared at Hoskins. "I'll make sure Cadet MacKenzie gets on the train. Leave. Now!"

Hoskins bowed up for a second, glanced at the captain then gave Jackson an evil smile. "See you later, MacKenzie."

Jackson swallowed. He was in for it now. Who knew how many calls he would get in the future. Hours of pushups and wind sprints in a quiet corner of the North area. Plus, Hoskins' favorite hazing ritual, a course of "Swim to Newburg" with him perched in freestyle position on the alcove rail, swimming until told to stop. If Hoskins knew Jackson was a member of the rock squad, meaning he was a terrible swimmer, he might get tossed headfirst into the Hudson River. Another one of Hoskins' favorites was a "White Tornado." Last week, he did it to Chris who puked after eating every condiment on the table. All of this despite the fact he received permission from his TAC officer, Captain Hickey. Hoskins wouldn't care. He loved to inflict pain and anxiety into Jackson's life like his private pet project.

After Hoskins stomped off, Captain Hayes placed a hand on Jackson's shoulder. "Is he one of the class bullies?"

Jackson nodded. "Yes, sir."

"Abusive?"

"He can be. The others cover for him. He's given some of the smaller plebes who have no experience in fighting back a few blanket parties. Especially those in the runt companies, A-2 and C-2. All I get is mental abuse and exercises to show me who's boss since I'm bigger than him and killed men in combat. One of my classmates wound up in the infirmary last week with a broken arm. Charlie told the staff he tripped in the dark coming back from the restroom."

"I'll take care of it. I'll recommend he be taken in front of the Commandant of Cadets for disrespecting Midshipman MacKenzie and me. It'll at least get him a few demerits and maybe some remediation. Something for him to think about the next time he starts to pull the same dumbass stunt."

"Thank you, sir. I've tried to report it but none of the upperclassmen would listen to me. I got quilled for speaking without permission."

"No problem. I'd rather weed out a bad apple than have a good one skewered by a worm. Enjoy a few minutes with your brother." Captain Hayes looked directly at Jim. "Make sure he gets on the train with his class."

Jim smiled. "Yes, sir."

Captain Hayes walked away, whistling *Anchors Aweigh*.

"How long do you have?" Jim asked.

Jackson looked at his watch. "An hour."

"Let's go find us a hot dog and a milkshake."

"Yes, sir." Jackson lightly punched his brother's shoulder. He was still leery of what might happen when he got back to the Point. Hoskins wasn't known for reining in his temper. He had lots of friends. Surely he wouldn't try something and bring on the wrath of a Navy captain after a very obvious warning. But you never knew. Hoskins was six donuts shy of a dozen.

December 1, 1953
West Point Cadet Barracks

Jackson looked up from his tactics class notes when two knocks sounded on the doorframe. "Room, attention," he yelled and jumped to attention at his desk. Chris did the same at his.

Commandant of Cadets, Brigadier General Watson, entered the room. He walked around, wiped his finger across a shelf, looked at it then dropped his hand. Then he went around the room. First, he tested the tightness of Jackson's bunk and the hospital corners. Next he pulled Jackson's enlisted Ike jacket out of the closet. Looking it over, running his hand over ribbons and the rank on the sleeves. Basically, he was doing an afternoon inspection, a PMI. "At ease."

Jackson and Chris put their hands behind their backs.

"MacKenzie, did you have a run-in with Cadet Hoskins at the Army/Navy game?"

"Yes, sir." Jackson glanced over at Chris. *Where's this going?*

"Did he approach you and your brother while you were speaking with Captain Hayes?"

"Yes, sir. May I ask a question, sir?"

"Yes, go ahead."

"Did Hoskins complain?" Jackson asked.

"No, Captain Hayes did."

Just like he said he would. "What did the captain say, sir?"

"That Hoskins has been abusing cadets. Specifically, throwing blanket parties, and Cadet Buzzard's broken arm is the result of one. Did you tell him that?"

"Yes, sir. He asked me a direct question. I had to tell the truth."

"Good for you, son. Have you tried to tell anyone in your chain of command before this?"

"Yes, sir. No one would listen. I got marks on my demerit slip for speaking out of turn. Is that why Hoskins hasn't been around?"

"Yes, after Captain Hayes filed the complaint with me for the disrespect, I asked Cadet Buzzard what happened. He confirmed what you told Captain Hayes. When I asked Cadet Hoskins about the incident, he admitted to causing Cadet Buzzard's injury and turned in his resignation. He left yesterday."

That's why the meals and my study time have been quiet. "Please excuse my impertinence, sir, but good riddance."

"No, it's completely understandable. I'm glad it came to our attention now instead of later after more cadets got hurt."

"Yes, sir."

General Watson held out his hand. "MacKenzie, give me your demerit slip."

Uh-oh. Am I in trouble? Jackson handed the folded paper to him. *This can't be good.*

The general unfolded the demerit slip, marked an x across the page, signed it, then handed it back to him. "You now have zero demerits again.

Get a new form for your pocket notebook. You won't be spending hours marching for punishment you don't deserve. Understood?"

"Yes, sir." Now he could spend more time at the stable training and playing with his horse.

"MacKenzie."

Jackson wondered about the general's weird tone. "Yes, sir."

"Given how well you've conducted yourself, I'm going to recommend that you be given the temporary rank of captain, making you the company commander for Plebe Christmas. You've had some leadership training and shown that you can handle pressure under fire. Good luck."

Jackson puffed out his chest. "Thank you, sir."

"Don't thank me yet. Your workload over the holidays just doubled. Go see your company commander in an hour so he can go over what your duties will entail. I need to tell him the plan. I hope you're the soldier Captain Hayes believes you to be. It was his suggestion."

"Yes, sir."

"Remember, I'll be keeping an eye on you. Consider this the first test of your leadership skills. There will be many more to come."

"Yes, sir."

"Good night." General Watson exited the room.

Once the door closed, Jackson and Chris relaxed.

Chris sat at his desk and picked up a pencil. "Hope you didn't bite off more than you can chew, Captain."

Jackson sat down and picked up his history notes. He had an exam to study for tomorrow. "Me too." *Hope this doesn't send me to my doom. Korea will seem easy. I wasn't juggling six balls in the air at the same time. Only two.*

Hopefully, by his third-class year, he'd be in a little less debt too. At $78.00 a month in pay, and his cadet uniforms and textbooks already costing him a king's mint, added to the $7.40 laundry bill and the $1.60 for dry cleaning, his head was barely above water. He almost couldn't afford to spend two dollars on snacks at Boodlers. Five cents for a candy bar and twenty-five cents for ice cream were practically unaffordable.

December 24, 1953

Jackson sighed. His written general reviews were over. He looked out the barracks window as snow fell across The Plain. The post was covered in a blanket of white. Here he was on Christmas, alone again. This time he was in the states, but he still couldn't visit his godparents. Plebes weren't allowed to leave the West Point grounds for Christmas.

Maybe that was a good thing. The letter from Aunt Sara in his Christmas care package of cookies, candy bars, underwear, t-shirts, and socks said nearly two feet of snow fell in Beaver Creek last week. That was four times as much as here in New York.

He wrapped his fuzzy cadet bathrobe tightly around his body. On his desk sat a small cardboard Christmas tree he made himself and decorated with bits of foil and twine. It wasn't any better than the scraggly pine tree in Korea.

His mom always demanded a big pine tree in the living room. She decorated it with red and green garland, blinking lights, and multi-colored ornaments, most of them handed down by her parents. Jim got to hang the ornaments.

Jackson's job was to put the star on top of the tree. When he was a toddler, his dad lifted him above his head so he could reach. As he grew older, he used a ladder to secure the star atop the tree. That was always his part of their Christmas tradition. One that he didn't have anymore. And would never have again. The star on his little tree was a West Point cufflink.

He pulled a chocolate chip cookie out of the box on his desk and munched on it. Nothing could beat Aunt Sara's cookies. Dinner was better than in Korea. Roast beef, potatoes, corn, and apple pie. Not that it helped his mood. At least it wasn't a mess hall staple, donkey dorks—rolled, stuffed meat substance.

Jackson heard the door open and close but didn't look. He knew it was Chris from the footsteps. With almost no upperclassmen around, he didn't have to worry about inspection on Christmas Eve. Right now, as a temporary captain, he was the highest-ranking cadet on the floor and in charge of the company. Trial by fire was right. But at the moment, he didn't care. Not at all. His official duties could wait until tomorrow.

"Hey, JJ. Want to go with me to the chapel?"

"Nah. I'm staying here. Too cold and too lonely."

"It might make you feel better."

"No, Mom and Dad always went to mass on Christmas Eve. I can't right now. Just can't."

"You know I understand."

Jackson looked over his shoulder. "Yeah, I do. But I still don't want to go. Maybe tomorrow, but not tonight." He pointed at the box. "Have a cookie. They're delicious."

Chris pulled out a cookie and took a bite. "Mmmm. Yeah, they are. Your aunt's a good cook."

He nodded. "Sure is. Aunt Sara makes the best sweet potatoes with pecan streusel, and my mouth waters just thinking about her pies. I have to wait another year before I can have a real Christmas with them. Did you get anything?"

"Yeah, my Aunt Charlotte sent me a new jacket and some cookies. They aren't as good as these."

"It's hard to be alone, Chris. I always wonder…"

"What?"

"If I had gotten that pass and gone to see Mom, would she have gone to the front? Would she have risked her life? She was less than a month from going home."

"Don't beat yourself up. You already know the answer."

"Yes. She would have. That's the MacKenzie way. Do your duty."

"From everything you've told me about her, you're right. I bet our parents are looking down on us from above right now, saying *be happy*. Don't dwell on what you can't change. Move forward to the future. It's the bright light ahead of you."

Jackson smiled. He could hear his mom saying exactly that. "True."

"I'll ask again. Do you want to come with me?"

"No, I can't. Too many memories I have to work through."

"Of what?" Chris pulled on his long overcoat.

"The war, Mom and Dad…stuff."

Chris grabbed his service cap off the dresser. "Okay. I'll be back in an hour, then let's play poker. I need to talk about my mom and dad too. I miss them with all my heart. It hurts so much I'll never enjoy another Christmas with them."

"Okay. I'll get the cards and jelly beans ready."

"And coffee. Pull that percolator you got from home out of its SAMI hiding place and get it going. Unless you want me to scrounge up some pan-THER piss."

"No, thank you, not interested in watered-down citrus drink. I'll stick with the coffee."

"Fine by me. It's time to stay up and watch for Santa Claus."

Jackson laughed. "Yeah, right." He'd love to see eight tiny reindeer pulling a sleigh and Santa land on The Plain. He heard the bells in the tower ringing in the distance. *I wonder what angel just got their wings.* He wiped away a tear with his hand. Flying high to join his parents.

CHAPTER 14

August 13, 1954
Camp Buckner, New York

As Jackson readied his gear, helmet, and pack for the second day of a simulated tactical exercise, he thought about these last few weeks. Today he'd been assigned as an NCO of a ten-man squad and given a Thompson sub-machine gun instead of his M1. A big test of his leadership skills and use of this training. Both here and in Korea.

Camp Buckner was constructed around the one-hundred-forty-nine-acre Lake Popolopen, fifteen miles from West Point in the Catskill Mountains. It consisted of six old-style barracks and a mess hall built by World War II German POWs. Surrounding the lake, a forest of pine trees. It smelled like an overflow of Christmas.

Training had consisted of many things. An orientation in Armor. Tanks like the M4 Sherman, M24 Chaffey, and M26 Pershing were a godsend for the Infantry in Korea. And they made great rides when your feet hurt.

Jackson whole-heartily loved Artillery. It was a life-saver to many a soldier under fire. He was familiar with fire direction protocols after a four-day stint with the 64th Artillery battalion. Captain Heller assigned him as a temporary body. He crunched his right middle finger after loading a shell into a 155mm Howitzer by slamming the breech block door on it. Ouch. His fingernail popped completely out, and the top of his finger turned black. It still hurt thinking about it as he hopped around like a chicken and spent a day in the infirmary.

The Signal Corps, well, not on his branch list by any means. Needed, yes, so they could communicate with each other in support of tactical operations, but...he knew all he needed to know.

The engineers showed them land navigation, which he learned in basic training. He managed to make his way along the Jamestown line with a map and compass. Now, the demolition part, blowing stuff up, he enjoyed. Turning big things into little things in a matter of milliseconds was something he could sink his teeth into. Mines, he'd seen those up close. Deadly to both soldiers and non-combatants.

Weapons qualifications on the M1 Garand and Colt .45 caliber pistol were fun. At least for Jackson. Chris managed to get M1-thumb. While reloading an eight-round en-bloc clip, the bolt stop disengaged and slammed into his left thumb. He wound up with a huge crescent-shaped blood blister under the nail.

The favorite of everyone, the quartermaster and his daily supply of boodle to the cadet store. Yummy snacks always made everything better when you were out in the field.

Once they were released from training for the day, as yearlings, they had more freedom than plebes. They could enjoy themselves. Swimming, sailing, rowing, or canoeing on Lake Popolopen. Jackson stayed out of the water to avoid drowning. He chose to lie in the sun on the man-made white sand beach in his shorts to get rid of his farmer's tan. His arms were dark. The rest of his body, always covered with his uniform, looked like pasty bread dough.

At night they could watch an old movie at the camp theater or sit outside and converse like normal people. Music floated in the air from several radios. Jackson, Chris, Charlie, and several other classmates played poker by the light of the moon filtering through the pine trees onto a piece of scrounged plywood supported by plastic milk crates.

On Saturdays, they still had parades and inspection under arms with their M1s, but now in their all-white India uniforms with the yellow yearling pin on the shoulder epaulets. They were upperclassmen. Finally.

After transport by a deuce-and-a-half out to the training area for the day's exercise, he led his squad through the forest to a downed trunk of an enormous pine tree. Their mission, to take out an enemy machine gun emplacement manned by his classmates. Chris commanded that position for this exercise.

Jackson glanced over the top of the log. He could see the emplacement in the distance at the top of the hill with the barrels of four .50 caliber Brownings pointing out over the sandbags. Due to the angle, unless you looked directly down from that emplacement, his position was nearly obscured by underbrush. That was his advantage. A frontal assault was out of the question. They'd be mowed down before they made it twenty feet up the hill. He looked over at Cadets Charlie Buzzard, Mark Watson, Zeke Webb, Albert Cross, Tyler Albertson, Pete Epps, Nilo Steele, Parker Waiter, and Jeremy Hodges.

"Charlie, take your BAR and use that dried creek to our right for cover to make your way up to their right flank. Stay low. Tyler, you, Mark, and Zeke cover him with your M1s." Jackson had to keep from scratching at his face. The heavy camouflage grease paint made it itch. His hands were sweaty enough without that crap all over them.

Cadet Charlie Buzzard nodded. "Got it."

"Pete, you, Parker, and Nilo follow the downed trees on our left. Belly crawl up the hill. Get on their left flank. Jeremy, Al, and I will wiggle our way through the underbrush. Watch for me to give a flash with my mirror, wait thirty seconds, then hit them with everything. They'll have to reposition those 50s. Once they're occupied with you, we'll go over the top."

With a nod, the men went off on their assignments. Jackson and his two men wiggled their way through the underbrush. For the places too small to go through, Jackson carefully cut the thick stalks with his combat knife. The thorns sliced deep through his fatigues and into his flesh. He felt the blood on his skin soaking his fatigues and the sting of sweat in the open cuts. Time slowed as he inched his way to the top.

Once they emerged from the underbrush, he was directly under the machine gun emplacement. With his signal mirror, he flashed once to his right then left and waited. Thirty seconds later, all hell broke loose as his squad opened up on both flanks. Jackson could hear the mad scramble above him to move those heavy Browning 50s.

As he readied himself to move, his helmet came off and went bouncing down the hill. For a second, he froze. They were dead meat, but no one looked over the sandbags. With his Thompson sub-machine gun against his shoulder, he climbed over the sandbags with his men. Together they took out the four gunners.

Patterson backed up and tripped over one of his fallen men. With his Thompson empty, Jackson pulled out his combat knife. As he went on a downward stoke toward Chris Patterson's head, a flashing image appeared in front of him. The burned North Korean officer who died in the airstrike. He shook his head and placed the knife against Chris' throat. This was too much like Korea and he hated it.

The observer, Major Hargrove, raised his hand. "Exercise completed. Good job, Cadet MacKenzie."

Jackson looked up, trying to slow his ragged breathing. "Yes, sir." He held out his hand and helped Chris up. "You okay?"

Chris brushed himself off. "Yeah, but you, Al, and Jeremy look like you've been through a bloodletting. Did you get hit for real? I thought we were using blanks."

Jackson glanced down at his uniform. Instead of green, it was almost black with blood and sweat. Blood trickled from every hole.

Major Hargrove pointed at a medic standing nearby. "MacKenzie, Cross, and Hodges go get those cuts cleaned up. The rest of you, head down the hill and let the other team have a crack at this."

Jackson grabbed Chris' arm. "Could you find my helmet? It's about fifty feet directly under us."

Chris smiled. "Sure. Lost it, did you? Not acceptable, ten demerits."

"Yeah, I'll take my punishment at the poker game tonight," Jackson replied.

2300 Hours

Jackson lay in his bunk in the 3rd Company barracks, clad in a t-shirt and shorts. He stared at the ceiling, unable to sleep from the pain. The cuts all over him stung from the sweat that coated his body. The aspirin the medic gave him finally kicked in and he closed his eyes.

Explosions ripped through the air. Fireballs lit the night sky. Jackson opened his eyes to...nothing but the darkness of the barracks and the snoring of his classmates. It wasn't Korea but Camp Buckner.

Jackson got up, quietly slipped on his fatigues and boots, then went outside. He walked down to Lake Popolopen and sat at the water's edge. All around him, crickets chipped, and bullfrogs croaked. Lit by only the moonlight, he tossed pebbles into the water. All he wanted to do was think.

Behind him, someone cleared their throat. Jackson involuntarily jerked, his hands searching for a knife that wasn't there. Then he realized again, he was at Camp Buckner.

"MacKenzie, are you okay?"

Jackson recognized the deep baritone voice of Captain Hickey, his TAC officer. He looked over his shoulder. The captain was standing a few feet behind him with his arms crossed. "Yes, sir."

"Why are you out here?" the captain asked in a soft yet commanding tone.

"Can't sleep, sir," Jackson replied.

"Because of the cuts...or something else."

Jackson's shoulders slumped. He hated to admit this. "Bad dream, sir. Korea."

"Want to talk about it?" Captain Hickey sat beside him.

"Not really." Jackson skipped a rock across the water.

"Cadet MacKenzie, you've been in the thick of it. For you, it was innocence lost to violence. To more death than a seventeen-year-old should ever see. You were forced to become a man by the barrel of a gun under the horrors of war."

"Yeah...I...my squad...was on patrol. We came across an encamped Chinese company. The airstrike turned them into barbeque. The air stank of cooked flesh and sulfur. Their flesh fell off the bones as we buried them. Sometimes I wonder…" Jackson trailed off.

"Is it worth being a soldier?"

"Yeah, exactly."

"I've thought the same thing when I've had an attack of conscience after what I did and saw in World War Two. It's hard to look into someone's eyes as they die. To kill. A soldier's job is difficult. Ours is a profession in which we live for peace and steadfastly hope we never have to fight. Sometimes, unfortunately, it can't be avoided."

"I know, sir. We can only piece together our shattered souls a little at a time and hope to move forward."

"That's prophetic from one so young and old at the same time."

Jackson laughed softly. "Yeah, funny how war and death will do that to a man."

"Feel better?"

"A little. Maybe."

"Go back to bed, Cadet MacKenzie. Get some sleep. You still have a lot of training ahead of you."

"Yes, sir." Jackson stood, brushing off the pine needles stuck to his pants.

"When we get back to post, if you ever need to talk, come to my office. We'll do it in private." Captain Hickey pointed at the barracks where the rest of his class was still sleeping. "Not out here in public where it can be used against you. Understood?"

"Yes, sir." Jackson headed back to his bunk. He did feel better and a little sleepy. Sometimes a man just can't outrun his demons. And it's true that only the dead have seen the end of war.

CHAPTER 15

June 8, 1955
West Point Cadet Barracks

Yesterday was graduation day. The spring term was over. The class of 1955 got a sendoff worthy of royalty. American royalty. President Eisenhower, himself a West Point graduate, gave the commencement speech in the Field House. Even though he'd seen Eisenhower at the p-rade, Jackson didn't think his graduation could top being that close to a sitting President. An Army general. A hero of World War II.

Jackson could only dream of what that day would feel like as he placed his gray cadet uniform inside his footlocker with the rest of his academy clothing. That stuff he would put into storage for the fall semester. His fatigues and everything he needed for summer training, he folded neatly and put into his duffle bag. His second year at West Point had been quiet. Much better than the first one. He passed all his tests, both academic and leadership, with flying colors.

The best part of his yearling year, the Army/Navy game last November. Jim joined him and the Corps of Cadets in the stands at halftime. He proudly showed off his Midshipman First Class uniform with its Lieutenant's rank on the sleeves and his academy class ring,

Jackson felt obliged to recite the *Ring Poop* poem to him. "What a crass mass of brass and glass! What a bold mold of rolled gold! What a cool jewel you got from your school! ...May I touch it please, sir!"

Jim took off the ring and placed it on Jackson's right ring finger. The ring was too big for him, but it didn't matter. He got to feel what it was like to wear the symbol of a "ring knocker" for a few minutes." Next fall, the lowly plebes would serenade him with the *Ring Poop* poem.

Unfortunately, Jim brought bad luck with his Navy blue and gold. The Army victory cannon didn't fire as they lost to Navy 27-20, and the cadets sang first and Navy second. Afterward, Jim treated him to a feast. They stuffed themselves with hot dogs, peanuts, french fries, potato chips, and ice cream. Even though his stomach protested on the train trip back to post, it was still a fantastic day.

For all his hard work, he was named to the distinguished cadet list. He earned a Superintendent's Award for excellence with a 3.0 GPA. A star man. Along with it came the Commander's Award for Excellence in the physical program for winning three regional equestrian meets and a national one at the Kentucky Horse Park. He received a special cadet award from the track team, an engraved bayonet mounted in a shadow box. He filled in as the anchor leg on the 880-yard relay team at the NCAA championships when another cadet broke his foot. The team got third place.

In the coming fall semester as a Cow, he was corporal and a squad leader. Something that he was very proud of. It placed him in a larger leadership role. The more duties he obtained, the more he would learn. Even if he failed, he would learn from it. But he never intended to fail if it could be avoided. Murphy and his laws always showed up when you least expected it.

Chris approached him with a towel slung over his shoulder. "Where are you going for our leave time in Norfolk?"

"DC. Meeting with my brother before he reports to the *USS Coral Sea* as their new weapons division officer."

"That's right, he graduated yesterday."

"Yeah. I couldn't get away because of our WGRs, and the TAC said no." *His girlfriend got to pin on his butter bars since Uncle Manny was stuck in Puerto Rico on maneuvers.*

"Why are you going to DC?"

"We're going to Arlington to see our parents. Neither of us wanted to do it alone."

"Why didn't you do that last year?"

"We couldn't get our schedules to mesh with Camp Buckner and the p-rade for the Supe. Mom and Dad would want us to go together."

"You know I understand."

"Yeah." Jackson thought for a second. "After we get finished at Elgin Air Force Base, what are your plans until we have to report back?"

"Staying with my dreadful Aunt Jenna. Why?"

"How about we make a road trip out of it and have some fun. Do some fishing. Find an amusement park, maybe take in a baseball game or two? Eat hotdogs and ice cream. You game?"

Chris paused for a second. "Sure. Why not? It beats visiting my Aunt Jenna in Tennessee. I always leave her house smelling like mothballs and cigar smoke, and it won't wash out of my clothes for at least a month."

"Great." Jackson latched his duffle bag shut and placed it next to the door. The only things still on the dresser, his uniform and boots for tomorrow's trip with the squids.

June 9, 1955

Jackson lugged his duffle bag up the boarding ramp of the *USS Cambria*, APA-36. The attack transport was tied up at West Point dock on the Hudson River. He looked over the side of the railing at the water and shuddered. Swimming was not his strong suit. He'd been a perpetual member of the rock squad at West Point. He could swim just enough to keep from drowning. But he would never wear one of those dreadful Mae Wests. They made him look like a wuss.

Chris pushed him forward. "You're holding up the line."

"Yeah, yeah." Jackson stepped off the ramp onto the deck. His gut churned as he felt the boat rock under his feet. It told him a lot. His dad might have loved it, but the Navy life wasn't for him. He followed the sailor in front of him below deck to the troop compartment. One word described it—claustrophobic. With canvas racks stacked four high, chained to the ceiling, and end to end, now he understood what his father meant by "hot bunking."

After stowing his gear in the space provided, Jackson followed Chris up on deck. He watched the crew throw lines as the ship got underway. Once he got used to feeling the ship's movement under his feet, he relaxed and leaned against the railing next to Chris. "This is kinda fun."

Chris nodded. "Yeah. Dad loved to sail. He had this small boat we took up the lake all the time."

As the day wore on, the sky got darker and darker as menacing storm clouds rolled in. The wind picked up and brought up some chop. The waves went from inches to a foot quickly. By the time they reached the headwaters of the Hudson River where it met the Atlantic Ocean in New York Harbor, the waves were rocking the ship back and forth. It rolled one way so much Jackson could see the water ten feet from the gunwale before shifting back in the other direction.

One classmate after another leaned over the rail. Soon almost everyone standing on the port side was puking over the railing. Everyone, including Jackson, learned a valuable lesson—always know which way the wind is blowing before you hurl.

June 10, 1955 – Norfolk, VA

Jackson looked at the bright blue, cloudless sky as he disembarked the *USS Cambria*. The kind of warm day where you wanted to be on the beach soaking up the sun. Building sandcastles and watching the beautiful girls in bikinis. It was a damn sight better than last night, at least what he saw of it. He missed chow, spending most of the evening sick rolling around in his rack covered with a blanket and shivering. He didn't understand how he could throw up that much with nothing in his stomach. But he wasn't the only one. Seasickness sidelined most of his class. Some of them still looked green around the gills as they descended the ramp.

Jackson made his way to the street in front of the dock and set his duffle bag on the concrete.

Chris squeezed his shoulder. "Are you ready for this?"

"Not really." Jackson looked around. He didn't see Jim's truck anywhere. "Must be running late."

"Yeah, traffic around a base can be murder."

Suddenly everything closed in on him. Jackson forced himself to breathe. He smelled gunpowder then heard explosions and shook his head to clear his ears.

Chris put a hand on his arm. "You okay? Your face went white."

"Fine." Jackson sighed.

Chris tapped the side of his head with a finger. "Do you think about it?"

Jackson looked at him. "About what?"

"You know...the war."

Chris saw right through him. Jackson nodded. "The memories come and go. Sometimes it's a sound or a smell. Other times there's no rhyme or reason to it. They just happen. There are so many memories like photographs in my mind I don't want to remember. Then I feel guilty for thinking that because I made it home and so many others didn't. But it feels like a penance to honor their memory."

"Yeah, there are days I see my buddies lying dead in the snow and I can't sleep. I—"

"Get up and stand at the window. Seen you do it many times. You'll get that thousand-yard stare where you're looking so incredibly hard at nothing in particular. And the memories just play like a movie in your head. I get lost in those thoughts, too, and wonder if things will ever get any better or easier. It's the kind of hurt that a man feels down in the fibers of his being."

Chris smiled. "Sure is. And I hold out hope that remembering it will be easier in due time."

A 1946 rusty dirt brown Chevy truck pulled up and parked in front of them. Jim got out. He was huge. His biceps strained the seams of his gray polo shirt and his blue jeans looked painted on. Every muscle showed. "Hey, little brother, you look good. You've bulked up some more."

"Look who's talking," Jackson replied. "I thought Captain America was climbing out of that truck."

"You're Captain America, kid. He's Army." Jim patted his shoulder. "I'm Superman. I just need a cape."

Jackson and Chris laughed.

"You sure do." Jackson pointed at Chris. "This is my roommate, Chris Patterson."

Jim stuck out his hand. "Heard a lot about you in JJ's letters. Nice to finally put a face with the name."

Chris shook Jim's hand. "Same here. Glad to know you're real, not a figment of JJ's imagination. The way he talks about you, I did picture Superman."

Jim glanced at Jackson. "Really. We'll have to talk about that, right, Cadet MacKenzie?"

Jackson snapped to attention. "Sir, yes, sir, Ensign MacKenzie."

"Where are you going for your weekend leave, Chris?" Jim asked.

"Virginia Beach. Charlie's meeting his girlfriend there and she's bringing a friend."

"Have fun." Jackson smiled at his friend. "Hope she's pretty. Not a Grant Hall Suzie or a skag."

"Me too. So we can do some back seat bingo." Chris lightly pushed him toward the truck. "Go."

Jackson tossed his duffle bag into the bed and climbed in on the passenger side.

Jim put the truck into gear. "How was your first ride with the Navy?"

Jackson groaned. "You had to ask that."

"That good, huh? Don't worry, kid, it only takes a couple of days to get your sea legs. Remember, drink plenty of water. What ship are you embarking on for the rest of your sea duty?"

Jackson shook his head. That was so like his big brother and his sense of humor. "The carrier *USS Valley Forge*."

Four hours later – Arlington National Cemetery

Jim parked in the closest space in the parking lot. "Let's go."

Jackson exited the truck, went to the back, and sat on the bumper.

"Hold on a minute." Jim pushed the back seat forward and grabbed something. He shut the door and met Jackson at the tailgate. In his left hand, he held a bouquet of red roses, their mother's favorite flower.

"I got directions and a map from my advisor a few days ago." Jim pulled a piece of paper out of his pocket. "They're in section 33, near Roosevelt and Grant Drive."

"You're in command, Ensign MacKenzie. Doesn't the Navy teach you how to navigate by the stars? Just follow the map." Jackson checked the position of the sun and pointed. "That way is north."

Jim laughed. "Sure is. Follow me." He went to the road next to the parking lot.

They followed King Drive to Eisenhower Drive. When it connected to Roosevelt Drive, Jackson's heart began beating faster. The closer they got to Grant Drive, the harder it got to hold in his emotions. He didn't want to cry before they even saw the gravesites.

At the intersection of Grant and Roosevelt Drive, they left the road, walking between the rows of endless white marble headstones.

Jim stopped, holding up the map and lining it up with the landmarks around them.

Jackson looked at his brother. His cheeks were pink and damp, and his eyes shiny. He couldn't tell if it was sweat or tears. It was a warm day.

"This way." Jim pointed to the southeast. They walked side by side for a while, then Jim suddenly stopped. "Mom and Dad should be here somewhere."

Jackson inched his way around the headstones in front of him. The inscription on one under the Christian cross read, Kimberly Ann MacKenzie – Major US Army – Korea – Purple Heart, Silver Star -Nurse, Mother, and Angel- January 5, 1907 – June 26, 1952. Next to it was his father's. It read, James Peter MacKenzie Sr.– Colonel USMC-WWII, Korea – Medal of Honor – Navy Cross - Father, Friend, Hero, January 31, 1905 – June 26, 1952. "Here they are, Jim."

Jim came up beside him. He placed the roses at the base of their mother's stone. From his pocket, he pulled out a black box. He opened it and set it in front of their father's stone. "Dad, these are for you since you didn't get to pin me."

Jackson pulled his NCAA bronze medal from his pocket and placed it over the bouquet of roses. Next to the black box, he placed a set of his West Point corporal stripes. They were pinned together by the collar insignia of the rank, a gray and gold West Point Second Class pin, and a Marine Corps Eagle, Globe, and Anchor.

Jim put his arm over Jackson's shoulders and pulled him close. "You okay, little brother?"

"No. You?" Jackson leaned into his brother's side for the warmth. He felt so cold. The reality of their parents' deaths hit him hard. Being here made it real. So final. He missed them so much. More pain than his heart could take as the tears fell.

"No." Jim brushed away Jackson's tears with a gentle hand before wiping at his own.

Jackson gave him a small smile. His brother was usually more reserved. Even so, it hurt all the way to his soul that he would never see them again, except like this. Buried under green grass together with names and dates etched in marble. At least until that day, far in the future, when they were together again.

CHAPTER 16

April 1, 1956
West Point – United States Military Academy Stable

"MacKenzie!" Coach Benson yelled.

Jackson poked his head above Firefly's back in his stall. "Yeah, coach."

Coach Benson waved an envelope in his hand. "Guess what came today."

Behind Coach Benson stood the Superintendent of West Point, Lieutenant General Finley, and Commandant of Cadets, Brigadier General Watson.

Jackson exited the stall. "Is it from the US Olympic Committee?"

"Yes. You want me to read it? Or do you want to?"

Jackson bounced on his feet. "You read it." Excited didn't describe how he felt, elation mixed with anxiety. He was also a bundle of nerves, worried he didn't make the cut. That he failed. Both extremes had his stomach doing flip-flops.

General Finley and General Watson joined him.

Coach Benson opened the envelope and unfolded the letter. He cleared his throat. "Cadet MacKenzie, It's my pleasure to inform you of your selection to the United States Olympic Equestrian Team as an alternate for jumping and dressage. You are not part of the three-day eventing team since you don't currently compete in that event. Your tryout at the Olympic Trials from March 10-17 in Tryon, North Carolina, was impressive. Your riding was perfect and your horse even more so. The only reason for your appointment as an alternate is your obligations as a West Point cadet that make you unable to train with the team. You can't fly to Europe to compete in the scheduled shows until you complete your spring semester classes. Once that occurs, you and your horse will be flown to Stockholm. This was explained to your teammates. They are very supportive of your decision to serve in the United States Army. Again, congratulations. Signed Kenneth L. 'Tug' Wilson. President of the United States Olympic Committee."

General Finley slapped Jackson on the shoulder. "Congratulations. That's quite an accomplishment."

"Yes, sir. Thank you, sir." Jackson couldn't wipe the smile off his face.

General Watson shook his hand. "I applaud you for your hard work and doing the Black Knights proud."

"Yes, sir. I hope to do the same in Stockholm too."

"You will, Cadet MacKenzie. I'm sure of it." General Finley glanced over at General Watson then back at Jackson. "Even though I know this is not what you want, as of this moment, your roommate, Cadet Patterson, will be taking over your duties as squad leader. You will use the time to train for the Olympics when not otherwise occupied with classes, drill, and homework. Understood."

Chris will love that. "Yes, sir. Understood. I'm to train hard. What about my written general reviews?"

"I'll make the arrangements with the Dean of Academics for you to take them before the end of term. They'll give you any extra one-on-one instruction needed for the tests. You have to be in Stockholm no later than June 2nd."

"Why, sir?" Jackson asked.

"To clear the Swedish livestock quarantine."

"Yes, sir. Permission to ask a question?"

"Go ahead," General Finley replied.

"Since I know someone in my class was denied admittance to the Olympic swim team, why am I being given special treatment?"

"Several reasons. First, you have some high-ranking backers, who wish to remain nameless, that requested you be allowed to attend the games. The regular games start in November during the fall term. That's why your classmate can't go. The equestrian games are in June. Even though you'll miss summer training, your nameless backers feel your experience in combat as an NCO more than makes up for what that training entails. And it will be a valuable learning experience for you dealing with people from other countries."

"Understood. Anything else, sir?"

"Yes. Tonight you will report to my house in casual civilian attire for dinner to celebrate your selection to the US Olympic Team and...as First Captain starting in the fall semester."

First Captain? I'm going the be First Captain. "Yes, sir." *That's incredible. I thought it would go to Chris. And eating with the superintendent is a privilege only given to a select few.* If he was in seventh heaven before, he wasn't sure where he was now. The euphoria was intoxicating and surreal. As if he were dreaming while awake. There were so many aspects of that conversation that could be considered defining moments. It would take time for him to process when the shock finally wore off.

"I'll see you at 1900 hours." General Finely nodded to General Watson, and they left the barn.

Coach Benson placed the letter back inside the envelope and handed it to Jackson. "Here. Finish grooming Firefly and go get cleaned up. You don't want to smell like the barn while eating with General Finley."

"No, sir." Jackson stuck the envelope in his black and gold West Point warm-up jacket hanging on a peg outside the stall. He didn't want Firefly to eat it. The horse ate anything that wasn't tied down. He went back into the stall and stroked Firefly's blaze. "We're headed to the Olympics, boy. Make me proud."

June 17, 1956
Olympic Stadium – Stockholm, Sweden

Jackson sat in the section of the stadium reserved for his team. One word described his mood—disappointment. Instead of being down on the grass accepting a medal, he was watching a man, a team, from another country being honored. Three of them. Gold, silver, and bronze medals hung around their necks. The only worthwhile thing he had done in Stockholm, riding Firefly in the opening ceremonies during the Parade of Nations.

Normally, equestrian competitors didn't ride their mounts in the ceremony. Too dangerous. Since the only Olympians present were the riders and their horses, they did something different. It allowed him the opportunity to get his picture taken with Firefly in front of the Olympic rings. He ordered lots of copies in many different sizes. This was probably the only time he would ever be an Olympian.

The opening ceremonies were beautiful. Full of pomp and circumstance. Grandiose and lavish. The Swedish Royal family came into the stadium escorted by a squadron of Royal Svea Life Guards. They looked elegant and impressive in their blue and yellow cavalry uniforms astride magnificent chestnut horses. Just as red as Firefly. The Olympic flag was brought in by riders, draped between the horses.

Another rider on horseback made a circuit of the stadium then lit the Olympic cauldron. The torch caught fire quickly, and the symbolic orange flames flickered and danced as the crowd erupted into thunderous applause. Two runners in white vests emblazoned with the Olympic rings carried the flame to the beacons at the stadium entrance. The King of Sweden opened the games. A Swedish dressage rider from the 1936 Berlin Games took the competitor's oath on horseback. During this, there was some excitement. At least for the US team. One rider was thrown during all the excitement. Luckily, he and his mount were both unhurt.

Jackson had done the same thing he was doing now for the last week. Watching his teammates and other teams ride. Relegated to being a one-man cheering squad. A water-bucket holder for the horses during the competitions and cooling them out afterward. Cleaning muddy and sweaty tack then polishing it. Washing and grooming horses until their coats gleamed like the sun. Mucking stalls. Feeding duty. Every horse on the team, in addition to Firefly. Grunt work. Meaningful grunt work. But still arduous, back-breaking grunt work. Normally assigned to a groom or barn worker. His coach didn't want to bring in a local. He didn't trust them for some reason. Might be because Sweden remained neutral during WWII. So Jackson got the duty.

He would officially go down as a member of the team in the history books. But he never got to show what he and Firefly could do. What they could accomplish. Flying over the jumps and clearing them by feet. Dancing across the dirt flawlessly in the dressage arena. The best the US team did in Olympic competition was 5th place. Not even in the running for a medal. The courses were extremely tough and the inclement weather conditions didn't help. There were periods of heavy rain. His rain slicker got a workout and he wound up soaking wet anyway. He knew in his heart, if given the chance, he and Firefly could have stood on that podium accepting a gold medal for the United States.

With so many people from different countries around, he practiced his German, Russian, and Spanish language skills with his fellow riders. Other than the opening ceremonies, that was the best part. Learning about their countries and horses. Their food and customs. Many of them were soldiers who wore their military uniforms during the competition.

Once the applause ended, the crowd stood and filtered out of the stadium.

The team coach pulled on Jackson's arm. "Come on, MacKenzie."

"Yes, sir." Jackson followed his coach down the aisle.

Coach stopped and turned. "I know you feel underappreciated. I know you wanted to compete, not be our lapdog…and you have every right to feel that way. We took advantage of you. You're the youngest man here and a rookie."

"Yes, sir."

"You did a great job. Did everything we asked and never complained. And with what happened during the competition, seeing how hard you train and how good your horse really is, I should've at least considered giving you a chance. Especially in dressage. You're better than anyone on our team or the others."

"But that's water under the bridge, right, coach? We can't go back in time and change it."

"Yeah, but after watching the dressage competition and who won…you could've beat him hands down. Remember that."

Jackson smiled. That made him feel better. "I will, sir."

"You have a future in this sport. At least consider it after you finish your obligation to the Army. I'd love to have you under my wing again. If you do, I promise you'll stand proudly on that podium accepting a gold medal for the United States of America."

"I will, sir. But that's a long time from now." Five years. And not likely to happen. He wanted to follow in his father's footsteps and serve as a military officer.

"Yes, it is. Let's go. We have a lot of work to do."

Jackson fell in behind his coach as they followed the crowd out of the stadium.

They did have a lot of work to do getting the horses ready for the trip home. Packing equipment, blankets, food, and water. Wrapping their legs for protection and booting their feet. Not to mention their own personal luggage.

He hoped nothing would happen. Horror stories were floating around about horses going crazy and being put down midflight to avoid injuring the others or their handlers. He wasn't worried about Firefly. That horse could take anything. Cold as ice. He slept the entire trip from the US to Sweden. He didn't want to watch one of his teammate's beautiful animals destroyed and stare at the body for the rest of the flight home. That would break his heart, and it had already been broken too many times.

June 26, 1956
United States Military Academy - West Point, NY

Jackson drew a deep breath as the truck pulling the horse trailer carrying Firefly entered the West Point grounds. Home. He was ready to get back into a normal routine. Waiting the three days with his teammates at the quarantine facility for their horses felt like forever. Years. A prison. Everyone slept in their horse's stall. Fed, watered, and groomed them. Unwilling to leave them alone in the care of the USDA and its underpaid lackeys.

Once he had Firefly settled, he would shower, change into his uniform, then join the West Point command staff at the administration building. Today he assumed his duties as First Captain. When the cadets returned from training, he had to meet with the brigade officers. They had to get ready to welcome the incoming new class of plebes on reception day.

This year, he was one of the cadets in the red sash. He couldn't wait to give the plebes hell by yelling, "Step up to my line. Not on my line. Not over my line. Report!" Revenge shouldn't be this sweet, but it sure would be. He'd been waiting for three years to do this.

As the stable came into view, Jackson was taken aback. Hundreds of people stood next to the fences. A black and gold banner that read, "Welcome home, Cadet MacKenzie and Firefly," hung from the trees.

When the truck stopped next to the pasture, Jackson climbed out. Lieutenant General Finley, Brigadier General Watson, and surprisingly, Major General Walker approached him.

Bet General Walker's one of my nameless benefactors. Jackson came to attention. "Sir."

Lieutenant General Finley shook his head. "At ease, Cadet MacKenzie. Not today. This is your day, not ours."

"Yes, sir." Jackson relaxed. *My day?*

Coach Benson joined them. "Can I have Cadet Tolson get Firefly out and walk him around to stretch his legs?"

"Please. It's been a long drive. Then take him out into the pasture on a long lead and let him graze for a while. I don't want him turned loose until he settles down. I'll relieve Tolson once I'm done. Thank you, sir."

"You're welcome."

Jackson pulled a folder out of the truck. He handed the pictures in cardboard sleeves to the three generals. "This is a picture of us in front of the Olympic rings."

General Finley nodded. "I'll have it framed immediately and hung in the administration building. I'll send a copy to the local paper for tomorrow's addition. Congratulations, Cadet MacKenzie."

"For what, sir? We didn't get to compete."

"For displaying the character of a West Point cadet and a future United States Army officer. I got a call from your coach. He couldn't say enough about how hard you worked to help the team without complaint, even though you didn't get to ride. He also said if he'd given you the chance, the United States would've brought home two gold medals from Stockholm."

"Thank you, sir. When do I need to assume my duties, sir?"

"Tomorrow. Meet me in my office at 0800 and we'll go over reception day. Today, get your horse settled and yourself too. No saluting. No uniforms. Understood?"

"Yes, sir."

General Walker held out his hand. "Great job, MacKenzie. I knew you'd do us proud and I'm proud of you, Trooper. Hope to have you back under my command someday."

"Yes, sir. I would be honored to serve under you again."

General Walker pulled a pen from his pocket. "Do me a favor before I leave?"

"What's that, sir?"

"Sign this." General Walker held out the cardboard sleeve.

"Sure, sir." *My first autograph.* He pulled out the picture, signed his name at the bottom, returned it to the sleeve, and handed it back. "Anything else, sir?"

"Yes." General Walker hugged him then stepped back. "Thank you for being the true person of character you showed in my office. You will go far, young man. I look forward to attending your graduation next year. If I can't, welcome to the United States Army." He held out his hand.

It took a second for the words to sink in, then Jackson shook the general's hand. "Thank you, sir."

General Walker nodded and walked to a green limousine flying the red flag of a two-star parked a few yards down the road.

Brigadier General Watson approached him. "Congratulations, Cadet MacKenzie. We'll take our leave of you now. Go take care of your horse."

"Yes, sir." Jackson came to attention.

"Your day, remember," General Watson admonished. Without another word, he left with General Finley.

Jackson relaxed. He grabbed two more photographs and handed them to Coach Benson. "One is for you. The other is for the stable wall."

"Thanks, Cadet MacKenzie...Jackson, you did good. I'm proud of you."

He's never called me by my first name before. "Sir?"

"Your day, remember. No salutes. Today, I'm Tom. Let's go see Firefly. I have a bag of peppermints and sugar cubes for him."

Jackson nodded. "Yes."

As they headed to the pasture, the cadets crowded around them, wanting to know everything about his Olympic experience. Including reporters from the cadet newspaper, *The Pointer View.*

"MacKenzie!" Cadet Hartman, a member of his class and defensive captain of the football team, yelled over the crowd.

"Yeah, Hartman." Jackson stopped and waited. Everyone around him parted to let the six-foot-five, two-hundred seventy-pound defensive tackle come forward.

"You think you're all big and bad, huh? Member of the Olympic Team. You didn't do anything, just worked as their errand boy. Tells me they considered you the same thing I do. A loser."

"Whatever, Hartman." He didn't like Hartman. The man was a typical jock. Tough on the outside with mush for brains.

"Just wait. You'll slip up one of these days." Hartman grabbed Jackson's arm. "Then you're mine, and I'll take my rightful place as First Captain."

"Only in your wet dreams." Jackson pulled his arm from Hartman's grasp.

Chris Patterson shoved Hartman back. "Let's go, buddy. That special horse of yours is looking for you."

Jackson glanced at the field. Firefly's head was up, his nostrils flared with his ears laid back. He was stomping his front feet. The horse probably felt the tension between him and Hartman. Jackson brushed the grip marks from his sleeve. "Remember, when classes start, I'm at the front of the brigade. You're in command of one of my companies. See you on reception day."

Hartman glared at him and stomped off.

"He's a sore loser. You'd better watch your back. His football buddies might give you a blanket party," Chris Patterson said.

"Only if he wants a one-way trip out of here for assault." Jackson pulled a handful of peppermints out of his pocket. "Come on, Chris. I'll teach you how to feed him." *Chris is right. Hartman might try something. And maybe get away with it since he's a pre-season All-American candidate. Better keep my guard up for a while.*

CHAPTER 17

October 21, 1956
West Point Cadet Barracks

Jackson looked up from his desk when Chris entered their room. He nodded and went back to his homework. Tomorrow he had to present his paper on the Battle of Okinawa. Uncle Manny had sent him his father's letters and the after-action reports to help with the presentation. Lots of facts that were not in the lectures given by his instructor. Things only the men who fought there knew. His father and Uncle Manny. The one thing he would leave out, his father's Medal of Honor. That he wanted kept a secret.

Chris sat on Jackson's bunk. "I need to talk to you."

"Sure." Jackson put his pencil down.

"Cadet Sterling filed a complaint with the Honor Committee."

"On who?"

"You."

"What?" Jackson slammed his hand on his desk. "Can you tell me why?"

"You cheated on the engineering exam last week."

"He's a yearling and not even in that class."

"I know." Chris leaned back on his elbows. "You sent him to remedial training and gigged him on the last inspection."

"So it's revenge. What did he say I did?"

"You stole the answer sheet from Captain Perkins' office. You could get separated from the academy if you can't prove otherwise."

Jackson stood and walked around the room. He picked up his tar bucket from the shelf and dusted off the brim with his sleeve. "True. And he knows this how?"

Chris pointed at the wall clock. "He saw you leave the barracks at 2100 through his window last Wednesday."

"Captain Perkins' office is on the other side of the post. How did he determine I stole the answer sheet? Did he follow me?"

"No, he said you came back with a folder in your hand."

Jackson cocked his head. "And that proves what?"

"Nothing, but you did have a perfect score on that test."

"Again, what does that prove? I've had perfect scores on the last three. I studied my butt off. I've only missed one question all semester. You have

140

to work the equations longhand and come up with the answer. That's kinda hard to fake without knowing the math."

"True. You're still going to have to go before the board." Chris chewed on his lower lip. "I'm taking your spot."

"Isn't that a conflict of interest?"

"The command representative could determine that it is. But…"

"We all do our duty no matter the consequences. I know."

"What was in the package?"

Jackson went to his desk and picked up a bundle of papers. "This. It's for my research paper in tactics. The librarian gave me copies of some microfilm records. She told me to come by and get them at 2130 when she closed up for the evening."

Chris nodded. "I believe you, but you have to prove it to the board."

"Yeah. Has Captain Perkins weighed in on this?"

"Not yet. The board will ask him at the hearing. Two of them are in that class."

"Uh-huh." Jackson crossed his arms. "Hartman flunked the test and has to take it over. I'm sure he won't be very supportive. He believes he should be First Captain. The jerk might find me guilty to make his bid to the commandant to get selected for the rest of term."

"And violate the Honor Code?" Chris questioned.

"Yes. Hartman's a slug. He's sliding by on everyone else's back. Doing only what he has to. If there was anyone I'd pick to be cheating, it's him. He passed the first three tests and failed this one miserably. I have no idea how he even got selected to the academy."

"Yes, you do. He was an all-star tackle in high school."

"And dumb as a post. He should be majoring in athletics, not engineering." Jackson sat at his desk. "Thanks, Chris. I have a paper to finish." He went back to his notes and started writing. This was more important than the board. He had the truth on his side. Even so, the thought that he might get kicked out for something he didn't do made him nervous.

October 22, 1956
Honor Board Hearing Room

Cadet Lieutenant Hannaford, the Honor Board Sergeant-at-Arms, stuck his head out of the doors. "They're ready for you, MacKenzie."

Jackson stood and straightened his gray jacket. He liked Greg Hannaford, an all-around good guy. Greg was a gifted musician. Every night, guitar music drifted down the halls an hour before lights out as he practiced. After a deep breath, Jackson marched into the room and stood before the board. "First Captain MacKenzie reporting as ordered."

The members of the board, all Firsties, were seated behind a long folding table. The Chairman, Cadet Epperson, Battalion Commanders Spindler, Dickerson, Connor, and Michaels, Company Commanders Newton and Hartman, and his Deputy Brigade Commander, the acting First Captain, Chris Patterson. Sitting off to one side, Lieutenant Colonel Martineau, the West Point Command Staff Honor officer.

Hartman had a pleased smile on his face. The others had no expression. *That can't be good.*

Epperson picked up a piece of paper. "These are instructions to the board so Cadet MacKenzie knows how this will be resolved. During this trial, it must be determined that there is reason to believe the violation occurred with clear and convincing evidence. The conclusion of guilt must not be based on guesswork, supposition, or conjecture. We don't require absolute certainty, only that enough proof exists to override every reasonable hypothesis except guilt. A guilty determination will require at least half the voting members plus one. Findings will be limited to guilty or not guilty. Votes will be by secret ballot. I'm responsible for counting them and announcing the verdict. If we find sufficient extenuating circumstances, the board can offer remediation. The vote for remediation will be conducted in the same manner as previously stated, except all members will vote for remediation or no remediation. I will be the deciding vote in case of a tie. Does everyone agree?"

Everyone seated behind the table nodded *yes*.

Epperson leaned forward. "Cadet MacKenzie. The charges against you are serious. It's a direct violation of two tenets of the Honor Code. Could you repeat that code to me?"

"A cadet will not lie, cheat, nor steal," Jackson said. As he spoke, those words reverberated off the deepest parts of his being. Those tenets were a part of his character long before he ever climbed the steps of the United States Military Academy. His parents would strike him down from above for breaking them.

"You've been accused of cheating on a test or tests and stealing the answer sheet and/or copying the test sheet by Cadet Sterling. How do you plead?"

"Not guilty."

"So noted. Do you want representation by another cadet as trial counsel?"

"No, sir. I'll represent myself."

142

"Noted. Let's begin. Where were you coming back from on 18 October after 2100 hours?"

"The library. I made arrangements with Miss Lovell to pick up some copied microfilm to use for my research paper."

"She is on the witness list and we'll be talking with her. Can you explain how a copy of the test questions with the answers was found in the barracks trash the day after the test?"

"No, sir." *Really?* "Everyone has access to the trash dumpster."

"True. But you're the only cadet accused of cheating on that test. Since the physical plant is behind on burning the trash, we're sifting through it to see if copies of other tests show up."

Shit! They really think I'm guilty. "Not from me, sir."

"Can you explain your perfect scores on the last three exams?"

"I studied hard for them." Jackson eyeballed Hartman. "And paid attention in class instead of sleeping."

Hartman glared back at him. "What does that mean, MacKenzie?"

"Only what I said. Take anything else up with Captain Perkins. I'm not the one getting a free ride for being a jock. Captain of the football team. Hah. Maybe peewee league."

Hartman stood from his chair, clenching his fists. "You little weasel. Can't wait to take your spot in front of the brigade. The only thing you did at the Olympics was embarrass us. I'll throw a party when they kick your sorry ass out of the academy."

Patterson pulled Hartman down into his chair. "Enough! Keep this focused on why we're here. Hartman, you act like an officer in the United States Army, or I'll have you replaced by someone else on the Honor Committee list. MacKenzie, you bite your tongue. Only answer the questions asked. No showboating. Understood?"

"Yes...sir." *He's doing his job. Wouldn't ask anything less. At least I got Hartman to show his true colors.*

Epperson tapped on the table. "Something else, MacKenzie. Cadet Sterling stated that when you returned, he went by your room and smelled the odor of a mimeograph machine."

"Well...yes. The copies from the library, remember, sir?"

"Of course. Anything to add in your defense?"

"Only that I'm innocent and have done nothing wrong, sir. I'm being framed for something I had no part of." *Don't like his attitude. He thinks I'm guilty too. Shit.*

"Your statement is duly noted by the board. We have other witnesses to interview. Go to class. You'll be notified when to return for the verdict. Dismissed."

Jackson came to attention. "Understood." He glanced at Patterson who nodded, then did a precise about-face and left the room. Before exiting the building, he looked at the clock. 1410. He had five minutes to get his tactics class to give his presentation. At least that he could prove it came from sources even his instructors didn't have access to. Who knows? Speaking in front of the class might be the last thing he did as a West Point cadet if no one came forward in his defense or they believed Sterling's lies. Hartman wielded a lot of power as captain of the football team. If that happened, he needed to go out in style. Proud. Head held high. Knowing that he was completely innocent.

Administration building
United States Military Academy - West Point, NY

After class, Jackson went to see his academic advisor, Major Paxton. He had to have more information than what the board told him, which was close to nothing at all. A test was found in the trash. How? Why would someone look in the trash? Go through the old, nasty garbage? Something was very wrong. And he had nothing to do with it. Time seemed to crawl as he waited for Major Paxton's secretary to announce him.

Mrs. Wright exited the inner door. "You can go in now, Cadet MacKenzie."

"Yes, ma'am." Jackson marched in and stood in front of the desk. "Cadet MacKenzie requesting permission to speak with you, sir."

"At ease, MacKenzie." Major Paxton put the paper in his hands on the desk. "Is this about the accusation by Cadet Sterling and the Honor Board hearing?"

"Yes, sir." Jackson put his arms behind his back. "I was wondering if you know more about it."

"I do, but I'm not at liberty to tell you at the moment."

"Why, sir? I did nothing wrong."

"Again, Cadet MacKenzie." Major Paxton slammed his hand on the desk. "I can't tell you anything. You'll have to wait until the Honor Board finishes interviewing the witnesses and renders their verdict."

"But sir…" Jackson winced. He didn't like this one bit. His dream could disappear in the space of just one lie. Poof. Up in a puff of smoke.

"You've been a member of the Honor Board as First Captain so you're familiar with how the system works."

"Yes, sir." Jackson glanced at the papers on the desk, trying to see if anything was about him.

Major Paxton closed the folder. "MacKenzie, nix any thoughts you have about looking into this yourself. You say you're innocent. If that's true, don't jeopardize being found as such by committing an honor code violation."

"What if I find the evidence to clear my name? And who's the one doing the cheating."

"Doesn't matter. If there's evidence, the board will find it." Major Paxton's expression turned to stone. "You won't do your case any good if you commit an honor violation or break one of the regulations to prove yourself innocent of another honor violation. Don't even think about going into Sterling's room and confronting him or interviewing any witnesses. That will taint anything you find out. You'll wind up in the same place you are now. In front of the board and most likely packing your bags to leave. Understood?"

"Yes, sir."

"I know waiting is hard, MacKenzie." Major Paxton took a deep breath. His facial expression softened. "You worked your butt off to get here. Served this country in a war zone. Then doubled down at the academy, doing twice the work and activities as most of the brigade. I don't know when you manage to sleep, you have such a tight schedule. But, that being said, follow the words of William Langland."

"What's that, sir?"

"Patience is a virtue. The ability to wait for something without getting angry or upset is a valuable quality in a person. Show us you have that quality. Show us that you are the United States Army officer your backers like General MacArthur and General Walker believe you to be. Go to class, do your homework, and complete your duties. Even though you're temporarily in Cadet Patterson's slot, make sure everything gets done." Major Paxton gave him a slight smile. "Capiche?"

"Jawohl."

Major Paxton laughed. "Nice." He checked the clock. "You need to get to the stable to take care of the horses and practice with the team. You have a meet coming up. Go on. Get moving."

Jackson snapped to attention. "Yes, sir." He turned and went to the door.

"MacKenzie."

Jackson looked over his shoulder. "Yes, sir."

"Keep your chin up. Everything will be okay. Trust the system. It's served us well for a hundred years. We don't kick out cadets who've done nothing wrong. If it happens by some volition of the cadets, you have the right to appeal the decision to the Commandant. Don't let it get you down. In the end, the right decision will be made."

"Yes, sir." Jackson nodded, straightened his jacket, and left the office. He had no choice but to wait. To violate the code to clear himself would only do more harm than good. Not only would it mar his character but also make him a hypocrite. Getting kicked out was unthinkable, but getting kicked out for something he brought on himself wasn't an option. He despised the feeling of helplessness he had in not controlling his own fate. He had been deliberate and calculated with every decision about his future that he had made up to this point. To have that control wrested from his grasp through was no fault of his own was nearly unbearable.

October 24, 1956

Jackson paced in front of the hearing room. Sweat rolled down his back. It had been two days since he stood before the board. His roommate and best friend since day one of the academy, Chris Patterson, had stayed in temporary housing instead of their room. His only contact with him was in class, meals, and formation, where he stood in a different spot. Not in front as First Captain.

Chris wouldn't speak to him. Only a stiff, formal nod or glaring eye contact. That was the same attitude from the rest of the brigade as well. They shunned him like a leper. Only speaking to him when absolutely necessary. Refusing to eat with him. He floated around the mess hall, looking for an empty seat. None appeared. Hungry, he accepted a full plate from a waiter and ate standing in a corner.

His instructors were a little better but not by much. It seemed everyone assumed he was guilty. Those reactions didn't bode well for what was about to happen. This very well could be his last day at West Point. Separated for an honor code violation.

Cadet Lieutenant Hannaford opened the doors. "They're ready for you, MacKenzie."

Jackson took a deep breath, composed himself as best he could, straightened his jacket, and went inside. He stopped in the same place as the last time, directly in front of Epperson. "First Captain MacKenzie reporting as ordered." He was First Captain and would announce himself as such. He did nothing wrong.

Epperson nodded. "At ease, Cadet MacKenzie."

Jackson spread his feet shoulder-width apart and put his hands behind his back. He looked around the room. Captain Perkins and Lieutenant Colonel Martineau sat in chairs against the wall with Lieutenant General Finley and Brigadier General Watson. In front of him, the same panel as before…except Hartman's seat was empty.

Epperson stood. "First Captain MacKenzie, the board finds you…not guilty. You are exonerated of all charges."

Captain Perkins walked over to Jackson. "Wondering what just happened?"

Jackson nodded. "Yes, sir."

"You were never a suspect in the thefts of the tests. So it shocked us for Cadet Sterling to name you specifically. We did have a suspect. For the last test, I prepared two. The one you took in class and a fake one."

"A fake one, sir?"

"Yes, I put the stencil for it in the same place I always do with the answer sheet under the mimeograph machine in my office. Copies of it were made but not by you."

"Who, sir?"

"The only person who flunked the last test."

Jackson cocked his head. "Hartman?"

"Yes. When Sterling named you, we knew that something was very wrong. We had to find out why. After some research, the administration staff found out Sterling and Hartman are cousins. Your poking the bear at the hearing gave us a reason."

"Hartman wanted to get rid of me."

"Yes, and throw any suspicion of cheating off himself. I'll have the results of this honor board hearing announced from the poop-deck at dinner to make sure the Corps knows the truth." Captain Perkins pointed at the table. "Take your rightful seat as part of the Honor Board, First Captain MacKenzie."

"Yes, sir." Jackson went around the table and sat in Hartman's empty chair.

Chris Patterson pulled on Jackson's sleeve. "Sorry for the deception. I had to keep you distant and confused to make it work. The Command Staff wanted Hartman to incriminate himself."

"You're a hell of an actor, my friend."

Patterson smiled. "And you're my best friend. Always."

"Okay. Now let's get down to business," Epperson said. "Sergeant-at-Arms, please send in the accused. Cadet Hartman."

1805 hours
United States Military Academy
Washington Hall

Unable to make it to dinner formation after a horse broke loose at the stable, Jackson straightened his gray wool jacket right outside the doors. The brigade had already entered Washington Hall. He tucked his service hat under his arm and went inside. Since most of the cadets still thought he cheated on the engineering test, the only people who would speak with him in class were members of the board. There wasn't any way to get the word out to everyone until now.

Jackson looked around the mass mayhem as nearly twenty-four hundred cadets took their places around the mess hall tables. The plebes assigned as gunner, and the beverage corporals stood at one end with the table commandant at the other. On both sides of the table between them, firsties, cows, and yearlings. He wondered if the gunner had his serving template tucked into his hat tonight. There would be hell to pay for the plebe if he didn't come prepared. Apple pie was on the menu for dessert.

Trying to find an open seat, Jackson floated around the north and southwest wing. Every time he located one, someone placed a book, hat, or something in the chair to block him from using it. Glares of contempt came from everyone he passed.

Resigned now to wait, Jackson drifted over to the poop-deck. He looked up and caught the eyes of Captain Perkins, who nodded back. The captain had seen what was going on.

The bonk, bonk, bonk, of someone tapping on the microphone to make sure it worked echoed over the voices of the cadets gossiping. "Attention everyone," blasted from the loudspeakers scattered around the wings.

An eerie quiet descended across the mess hall as all talking stopped and heads turned in his direction. Jackson felt like everyone's eyes were fixed on him. Even though he was innocent, it made him uneasy.

"I have an announcement to make," said Captain Perkins. "The Honor Board has come to a decision in the complaint against Cadet MacKenzie. He is innocent of all charges. A false accusation was leveled against him by Cadet Sterling. During the investigation, we discovered Cadet Sterling and Cadet Hartman had concocted a scheme to get rid of Cadet MacKenzie. Cadet Hartman wanted to make a bid to become First Captain.

We confirmed through evidence and witnesses Cadet Hartman snuck into my office and stole the tests and answer sheets. Both he and Cadet Sterling have been dismissed from the academy for breaking the honor code. Please welcome First Captain MacKenzie back to his rightful place as one of us."

Applause broke out in the hall, bringing a smile to Jackson's face. His honor was restored.

Chris approached him. "Need a seat, buddy?"

Jackson nodded. "Yeah."

"Come with me." Chris pulled on Jackson's sleeve.

Jackson followed him to a table in the southwest wing, directly in front of the battle mural. No one stood next to the table commandant's chair.

Chris stood next to the empty chair to the right of it. "Take your place, sir."

Jackson pulled out the chair and waited.

"Take seats."

Everyone sat down and scooted their chairs up to the table.

The waiter handed the Gunner, Cadet Black, a plate of spaghetti.

"Sir, the spaghetti with meatballs are on the table, spaghetti with meatballs for the head of the table, sir," he announced loudly, then passed the platter to Jackson.

Even though pasta and apple pie was a weekly occurrence, this dinner would taste extra special. Jackson accepted the platter, spooned out a large portion onto his plate then handed it to Chris. Now he was home.

CHAPTER 18

June 4, 1957
West Point, NY - United States Military Academy
Graduation Day - 1000 hours

Jackson stood at attention in front of the formation of 546 senior cadets on the floor of the Field House. All of them dressed in their fitted full dress gray wool jacket with 44 gold-plated brass buttons and swallow-tails. Worn with it, a white cotton cross belt with a centered breastplate over his right shoulder, white pants, black low-quarter shoes, and a red sash. On his left hip, attached to the cross belt, his cadet sword, issued to him as a plebe. His white standard dress hat glared in the overhead lights.

In front of him, a number of dignitaries. Ranging from Secretary of the Army Wilbur Brucker, generals, senators, representatives, actors, and businessmen. General Maxwell D. Taylor, Chief of Staff of the Army, gave the commencement speech. Somewhere behind him in the audience of ten thousand people was his godfather, Lieutenant General Mangus Malone, and Sergeant Major Jason Nichols. Both of them were the personification of professionalism and military bearing in their Marine Corps dress blue uniforms. With them, his godmother, Sara Malone, in her yellow summer dress and Aunt Janet Nichols in a green dress. Jackson's graduations from basic training and Airborne school did not hold a candle to the pageantry and tradition on display in the ceremony he was now taking part in. One thing dampened the day. Jim couldn't make it. The *USS Coral Sea* was on NATO maneuvers in the Mediterranean Sea.

Jackson thought about yesterday while the staff called the soon-to-be Army Second Lieutenants to the stage to receive their diplomas. Since it was alphabetical, it would take a while. The day started out fine. June week was always a time to meet with returning alumni and dignitaries. And he met quite a few at the Superintendent's reception.

During the graduation p-rade on The Plain, the day turned upside down. The parade went as rehearsed until it came time for the Firsties to join the reviewing line. They were supposed to step out from their company formations, march away from the Corps, and form a "Long Gray Line" in front of the bleachers. On command, they would perform an about-face and watch the remaining cadets salute them as they passed by on parade. It started out as planned then all hell broke loose. A large number of them did the unthinkable. They broke ranks. In a rambunctious flood, they ran to the reviewing stands, whooping and hollering as if they were leading a charge. A few got tangled up in their swords and took a header.

Jackson stayed in formation with the Brigade Staff as did his roommate, the Deputy Brigade Commander, Chris Patterson. The Regimental and Battalion staff remained mostly intact and continued to march. As did the senior members of companies I-1, L-1, L-2, and M-1. They stopped at the company standards at attention, saluted, and waited to be released. Once the order was given, he and those seniors joined the reviewing line with their rabble-rousing classmates. He was embarrassed, fuming, beet red, hot from his neck to forehead flustered, disconcerted, and ashamed. This was his second time to face the barracks in a pass in review. The first, when he joined the Brigade as a plebe four years ago. And it was a disaster.

With his tar bucket tucked under his left arm, its plume feathers fluttering in the breeze, Jackson watched the underclassmen go by in a pass in review. They were led by the class of 1958—the cadets who would take their place as Firsties in the fall.

Those who ran paid for it that night. Upon their return to the North Area, they were chewed out by their tactical officers and confined to their rooms. Then came the age-old Plebe "Clothing Formation" drill. A favorite during Beast Barracks. Changing into a different uniform for inspection by the TACs every twenty minutes. The offending members of the class were lucky the punishment wasn't more severe. The staff had considered several options. They did put the class in confinement. But they stopped short of delaying graduation, canceling the graduation hop, writing Article 15 letters of reprimand, or issuing fines. Instead, all were given a royal ass chewing in the Army Theater by General Taylor.

Those who stayed in formation got to leave campus and have a nice evening with their guests. And Jackson did after a private meeting with Generals Taylor, Finley, and Watson. They didn't chew him out but did let him know of their disappointment in his classmates' behavior. Afterward, Uncle Manny took him, Aunt Sara, Uncle Jason, and Aunt Janet out for a wonderful steak dinner. When he returned to the barracks, some of his classmates apologized for breaking ranks. That helped to ease the sting. After all, it wasn't the end of the world. Just an ill-timed prank that should've never occurred if someone has used their brain for something other than a rack for their tar bucket.

He had lost 201 of his classmates during his four years at the academy. Most washed out due to poor grades. Some failed the military training or physical part of the academy. A few of them got recycled to later classes. A small percentage couldn't hack being away from home and quit.

Then there was the asshole, Meyers Hartman. Jackson took great pleasure in announcing the recommendation of the board. Separation from the academy for an Honor Code violation. Hartman was gone the next day with his tail tucked between his legs. So was his All-American status and possible selection for the Heisman Trophy, Maxwell Award, or Outland Trophy. And a big-time NFL contract after his time in the Army was up. Now he had to give the Army five years in the enlisted ranks. Last Jackson heard, Private Hartman was cleaning latrines at Ft. Hood.

During his walk across the stage, Jackson's emotions welled up inside him. Happiness, euphoria, excitement, exhilaration, elation, and contentment all jammed together. As he accepted his diploma from General Taylor, he was also proud. He couldn't push his chest out any farther. He'd done what he set out to do, graduate from West Point with honors.

The final year had been tough. Harder than he thought it would be. He'd spent many a late night studying with his roommate Chris Patterson. Staying awake by eating pizza, candy bars, cookies, cupcakes, Twinkies, and drinking strong black coffee. His father's special concoction. It wasn't just the classwork. His other activities took a huge chunk of his time and sleep. The equestrian team, track team, the Olympics, and his duties as First Captain. The highest position in the cadet chain of command. He was responsible for the overall performance of the entire Corps of Cadets. His duties included implementing a class agenda and acting as a liaison between the Corps and the administration.

Through his hard work, he received a litany of awards. The Knox Trophy was awarded to the cadet with the highest ratings in Military Efficiency. The General William A. Mitchell Memorial Award for the highest rating in Military Engineering and History. The American Ordinance Association Award for the highest rating in Ordinance. The 306th Infantry Award for excellence in Physical Development. The General John J. Pershing Memorial Award for the highest rating in Military Science over the four-year course. The Superintendent's Award for Excellence by demonstrating outstanding performance in three programs: Academic, Military, and Physical.

The Distinguished Cadet Award for being in the top 5% of his class. He had a perfect 3.0. The Major General Francis Vinton Greene Memorial Award as the graduating cadet achieving the highest class standing. The Pershing Sword for serving as Cadet First Captain and Brigade Commander. The Eisenhower Award for Excellence in Military Psychology and Leadership. And the Men's Army Athletic Association

Trophy for his selection as an alternate on the 1956 US Equestrian Olympic team. The command staff determined he had contributed the most valuable service to Army athletics. It surprised him to get it instead of someone on the football team.

In all, he received a silver bowl for the Know Trophy. A gold star encircled by a wreath and an additional gold star for the Superintendent and Distinguished Cadet Award. Three silver trays for the General John J. Pershing Memorial Award, the Eisenhower Award, and the Men's Army Athletic Association Award. A pistol for the Major General Francis Vinton Greene Memorial Award. A rifle for the American Ordinance Award. A set of books for the General Mitchell Award. And a sword for the Pershing Sword. He needed an extra-large footlocker to hold everything.

"Please remain standing while the oath of office is administered to the class of 1957 and welcome the United States Military Academy Commandant of Cadets, Brigadier General Leroy I. Watson," came from the speakers mounted around the stadium.

Applause came from the audience.

My dream is finally here. I made it. Sweat rolled down his face. He couldn't wipe it away. Not while standing at attention on his final day at West Point. He twisted his academy class ring around his finger with his thumb. Given to him at Cullum Hall on Ring Weekend last September, the yellow gold ring bearing the West Point crest with a blue stone representing the infantry marked the beginning of the end. The ring slipped easily around his sweaty finger.

"Raise your right hand and repeat after me," General Watson said.

Jackson raised his hand with his class.

"I, state your name." The general paused.

"I, Jackson Joseph MacKenzie." It sounded like a garble with the rest of the class.

"Having been appointed an officer in the Army of the United States." Another pause from the general as the class repeated it.

"In the grade of Second Lieutenant do solemnly swear."

Jackson felt his heart beat faster saying the words.

"That I will support and defend the Constitution of the United States...Against all enemies, foreign and domestic...That I will bear true faith and allegiance to the same...That I take the obligation freely without any mental reservation...or purpose of evasion...and that I will well and faithfully discharge the duties of the office...on which I am about to enter...So help me God."

Jackson felt a weight both lift and land on his shoulders. He was no longer a cadet but an Army officer.

"Please lower your hand," the general said.

Jackson lowered his arm with his classmates.

The audience broke out in applause behind them.

The announcer returned to the microphone. "Ladies and gentlemen, please remain standing and join in the singing of the official Army song, 'When the Army Goes Rolling Along.'"

Jackson had to fight to contain himself singing with the band, audience, and classmates.

After the band and the vocals ended, Jackson faced his classmates. "Class...Un...cover."

The class removed their hats.

Jackson faced the stage, removed his hat, and cradled it on his outstretched left arm.

"Please remain standing for the benediction by Chaplain Klein," said the announcer.

Hurry up. Jackson locked himself at attention while the chaplain spoke. The ceremony was dragging on. He was ready for it to end and see his family. His godparents, and Jason and Janet Nichols. He placed his hat back on upon the command from General Watson to "re...cover."

"Commandant, take charge of the graduating class of the United States Military Academy," said General Finley over the loudspeakers.

General Watson saluted General Finley then turned to face Jackson and his classmates. "Second Lieutenant MacKenzie, dismiss the class of 1957."

Jackson saluted, turned, and faced his classmates. "Class...Re...cover."

The class placed their hats on their heads.

"Class of 1957...Dis..." He grabbed the brim of his cap. "Missed." Then he tossed the cap into the air with his classmates. They floated down everywhere. Now it was finally over.

Screams broke out, and the band started playing. Everyone hugged each other as families flooded onto the floor.

Jackson grabbed his diploma from his chair then elbowed his way through the crowd. Standing off to the side were two men in Marine Corps dress blue uniforms. Their chests decorated and adorned with multiple colorful medals. Trying to maintain decorum, he walked instead of ran to them.

As he approached, Jackson could see Sara and Janet had been crying. Their eyes were all puffy and red. Mangus and Jason's were too. They kept their faces somewhat in the stoic fashion of Marines.

Jackson stopped in front of Jason.

Jason came to attention and saluted.

Jackson returned the salute, pulled a silver dollar from under his red sash, and handed it to him. Tradition dictated the gift for his first salute from an NCO. Then he saluted his godfather.

Mangus returned the salute. "At ease...Lieutenant MacKenzie."

"Yes, sir." Jackson relaxed.

Sara held out her hand. "Give me your diploma so you don't have to hang onto it."

"Yes, ma'am." Jackson handed it to her. He looked around. Chris was nowhere to be seen. Probably with his girlfriend's parents. *I'll catch him at the banquet.*

"Your mom and dad would be so proud of you." Sara hugged him then kissed his cheek.

"I know." Jackson sniffed. He missed them so much. "I wish Jim could be here. He's in underwater demolition training in Florida."

"I tried, kid. But if he misses any time, he has to start over again."

"Wouldn't want to do that either." Jackson pointed toward the North Area. "Let's head to my room. I want to change. You have a duty to perform, General Malone."

Mangus laughed. "I sure do. Been waiting four years to do this."

One hour later

Jackson stepped out of his room dressed in his new class A Army green uniform with his service cap tucked under his arm. On his jacket over the left breast pocket were his ribbons. Army Distinguished Service Cross, Silver Star, Soldier's Medal, Purple Heart with oak leaf cluster, National Defense Service Medal, Korean Service Medal, and United Nations Korean Service Medal. Above that, his Combat Infantry Badge and Airborne wings. Over the right pocket, the Republic of Korea Presidential Unit Citation. Draped over his right shoulder, his blue infantry cord. On his right sleeve, two overseas service bars for his year of combat duty in Korea and a 25th Infantry patch on the shoulder.

Inside he was smiling. His orders had been stuck to the inside of his door. He was being sent to Fort Campbell, assigned to the 101st Airborne.

The historic Screaming Eagles. Once tradition was taken care of, he would tell everyone.

He led everyone to Washington Hall. The place of many good memories and a few bad ones. The West Point command staff would be hanging around since the buffet started at 1230 hours. This he wanted them to see. He wanted his secret to be revealed.

Out front stood Lieutenant General Finley and Brigadier General Watson. They were greeting the new officers and their families as they entered the hall.

Jackson smiled. He approached the two officers. "General Finley, General Watson. I want you to meet my godfather, Lieutenant General Mangus Malone."

They looked at Mangus, then Jackson, then back at Mangus.

"Hmm. You're Bulldog Malone. The commanding officer of the First Marine Expeditionary Force."

Jackson cringed. His godfather hated that nickname.

Mangus remained Marine cool. "Yes, I am."

"I didn't know Lieutenant MacKenzie had such a famous supporter."

"Not as much as his dad," Mangus replied.

"Who was his father?" General Watson asked.

"Colonel James MacKenzie. United States Marine Corps. Recipient of the Medal of Honor for the Battle of Okinawa and the Navy Cross in Korea," Mangus said proudly.

Jackson wanted to duck his head. He remained standing at loose attention. No one at the Point knew that.

The two generals' eyes widened.

"Do you want to witness this?" Mangus asked.

The two men nodded. "Yes, sir."

Mangus faced Jackson. "Attention to orders."

Jackson snapped to attention.

Mangus said the officer's oath, which Jackson repeated.

Sara put her camera to her eye and took pictures of them. He would have her send him a set to Fort Campbell for his scrapbook.

Jason and Janet smiled, holding hands. Their eyes said everything, bright, shining, and happy. They were proud of him.

Jackson kept his eyes straight ahead as Mangus pulled a black box from his pocket. He took the two single gold bars out and pinned one to each of Jackson's shoulder epaulets. Now he was officially a Second Lieutenant. "Congratulations, kid. I got the honor of pinning a MacKenzie."

"Yes, sir. General Malone."

General Finley and General Watson nodded and went back to greeting the guests.

Jackson pointed at the doors. "Let's eat. I'm starving. The day isn't over yet." He still had things to do. First, pack his personal belongings in Uncle Manny's car. Then came the mundane stuff. He had to sign out of his company, pick up his paperwork, return his issued equipment, and officially clear the post. That would take at least three hours.

Sara, ever the Marine wife, came prepared with a blanket, snacks, and a battery-powered radio. They would lounge by the water listening to music while waiting for him. With a month's leave coming before he had to report for duty, he intended to have fun and relax, like those two weeks with Chris in 1955. On his bucket list, ride the scariest amusement park roller coaster a dozen times. And take a flying lesson.

One thing bothered him about graduating, leaving his beloved horse, Firefly. He could only hope Firefly would find another cadet to bond with, to be loved by, and live the rest of his life in the safety and security of West Point. Coach Benson had assured him a gravesite in the cemetery was already reserved for Firefly with a military marble headstone engraved with his name and the Olympic rings.

CHAPTER 19

April 7, 1985
Harve, Montana Hospital

Jackson opened his eyes as a hand stroked his forehead. For a moment, he didn't know where he was, then he thought he was at the West Point in the infirmary, sick with the flu. The dream was so vivid, detailed, and real. His life. His past. The intense emotions hovered just beyond his grasp. In his heart. *I'm in a hospital. The snakebite.* He looked into his godmother's green eyes. "Hi, Aunt Sara. How long have I been out?"

"Hi yourself, squirt. About six days." Sara gripped his hand. "Someone else is here."

A blurred image with long red hair leaned over the bed. The scent of lavender filled the air. Jackson gripped the hand that latched onto his. "Hey, Cathy. Hope you're not mad at me?"

Cathy shook her head. "Of course not. Your doctor, however, is pissing me off. He won't let me see your records. Says it's in your best interest."

"You mean he's treating you as my girlfriend, huh? Not a doctor or an equal. Doesn't sit right when the shoe's on the other foot, does it?"

"No, it doesn't. Do you remember anything?"

Jackson spotted a paperback book on the table next to a Styrofoam coffee cup. "You've been reading to me, right?"

"Yes. Do you know what novel?"

"Not this time. I had a bizarre dream. What novel?'

"*The Warrior's Path* by Louis L'Amour? What kind of dream?"

"I was back in Korea. The war. West Point. It felt so real. Like I was really there. I felt the pain. The emotions when Uncle Manny told me Mom and Dad died. Lots of stuff. Some of the things I'd like to forget. Forever."

"You've been on several pretty heavy drugs for the last few days. Some of them can cause vivid dreams and hallucinations. You had so much paralysis in your face and neck from the venom, the doctor almost put a trach tube in your throat. Luckily, you started breathing better when the anti-venom stabilized your vital signs."

"Okay. It just felt so real. Did you finish the book?"

"Not yet." Cathy picked up the book. "Got twenty pages left."

"Then start reading." Jackson leaned back into his pillows with his hands behind his head. "I'm not going anywhere."

April 8, 1985 - 1100 hours

Jackson stretched and enjoyed the sun shining through the windows. His nurse removed the IV lines a few hours earlier after pulling enough blood to fill a blood bank.

Dr. Baker came in. "Ready to go home? Your blood work is normal this morning and your lungs are clear."

"Great." Jackson threw off his blanket then replaced it. *Oops, not wearing anything but a hospital gown.* He turned to Sara and Cathy. "I need some clothes."

Cathy pulled a small duffle bag from the closet. "And a wheelchair. When we get home, I'm the doctor. You do what I say, right?"

"Yes, ma'am." Jackson pulled on the underwear, faded Army Black Knights sweatpants, hooded sweatshirt, and house slippers she handed him. He sat quietly in the wheelchair as the orderly pushed it to the front lobby. No way did he want Cathy on his case in public. That would be embarrassing.

1300 hours – Double M Ranch

Jackson gazed at the cloudless bright blue sky through the Suburban's open passenger door. "It's a beautiful day."

Cathy helped him onto his crutches. "Yes. What makes it better is you're alive to see it."

Mangus held open the front door. "Get your butt inside."

Jackson hobbled into the lower bedroom and sat on the king-size bed.

Sara handed him a set of light blue pajamas. "Change into these. I'll bring you some chicken soup and crackers."

"Thank you. I'm hungry." Jackson pulled his sweatshirt over his head and tossed it across the headboard.

Cathy removed his slippers then eased off his sweatpants. "Until your leg returns to normal size, the only trip you make is to the bathroom. Don't even think about going to the barn without my permission."

Jackson paused at the top button of the pajama shirt. "But…Bandit saved my life."

"No. That leg is still swollen and your immune system is compromised. I don't need you catching a cold going into that germ-filled barn. You stay in bed. That's an order." Cathy shook her finger at him. "Remember, I'll be watching you."

"I'm sure you will be." Jackson leaned back into his pillows. He wanted to put the dream into perspective. To think. He hadn't thought about that time of his life in years. It was hard to put his parents' deaths behind him. His entire existence was shaped by them, even here at the ranch. This was their room when they visited. He sniffed. Somewhere in the back of his mind, he smelled Miss Dior and Old Spice.

April 11, 1985

Jackson checked the digital clock on the nightstand. 0400 hours. He snuck on his crutches past Cathy asleep on the living room couch. *Thank goodness for the soft carpet.* Each step was gentle and slow to keep his right leg off the ground. The shadows of the furniture helped hide his escape. So did the well-oiled door hinges. Ever so carefully, he hobbled to the barn. He didn't want to wind up back in the hospital by falling on his face.

Bandit stuck his head over the stall door and neighed. He shook his head. His long red mane flopped over his forehead between his ears.

"Hey, buddy." Jackson stuck a handful of mints under the horse's nose. "Thanks for saving my life." The door creaked then slammed shut. Light footsteps signaled someone's approach. *Uh-oh! Caught.*

"What are you doing?"

Jackson cringed at Cathy's shrill tone. She was mad at him. Really mad. He turned and leaned on his crutches. "I'm sorry, honey. I had to see him."

Cathy crossed her arms. "It's like herding cats to keep you in bed. I told you the rules and you chose to break them. Did you do that at West Point?"

She zinged him good. "No, of course not. I'd wind up doing area tours for hours."

"Thought so." Cathy pointed at the door. "Get your butt back into the house, mister, before I kick it back there myself."

Jackson dropped his head. "Yes, doctor." He hobbled back to the house. Slow enough to keep Cathy off his back. *At least I'm alive to be yelled at. I could be six feet under next to Bill.* Ever so carefully, he looked over his shoulder.

"I see you looking at me." She poked him in the back with her finger. "Keep moving."

"Yes, ma'am." *There goes my freedom. She'll be watching my every more. I've got more than one trick up my sleeve. My life since West Point had been one hell of a run. Hooah!*

Made in the USA
Columbia, SC
12 July 2021

41724110R00091